AF451300

Mating with Mothman

MrJ

WARNING

This work of fiction contains mature themes and situations that may be disturbing or triggering to some readers. Discretion is advised.

Trigger Warnings:
Explicit Sexual Content: The story includes detailed descriptions of sexual encounters, including oral sex and nudity.

Sexual Assault and Harassment: The story contains scenes depicting and discussing sexual assault and harassment.

Violence, Gore, and Physical Abuse: The narrative includes scenes of violence, gore, and physical abuse.

Kidnapping and Confinement: A character is kidnapped and held against their will.

Stalking and Obsessive Behavior: A character exhibits stalking behaviors and becomes dangerously obsessed with another character.

Emotional Abuse and Manipulation: The story portrays instances of emotional abuse and manipulation within relationships.

Alcohol Abuse: Characters engage in excessive alcohol consumption, and the narrative portrays the negative consequences of alcohol abuse.

Death and Suicide: The narrative references the death of a character and discusses the topic of suicide.

Sexism and Misogyny: The narrative contains instances of sexism and misogynistic attitudes and behaviors.

Body Horror and Transformation: The narrative features characters undergoing disturbing physical transformations.

This advisory is provided to ensure reader safety and comfort. If you are sensitive to any of the themes listed above, please proceed with caution or consider whether this book is right for you.

ISBN: 978-91-989544-0-1

Published by MrJ

Cover Design and illustrations: Yttepytte Design
Edited by: Macko Bole, Malva

CHAPTER 1

The shiny, navy blue truck that pulled her into the driveway was comfortable enough, even on the rough dirt roads surrounding Springdale. All the same, May was glad to step out. It had been a long trip from home. The mud squishing beneath the heels of her simple brown boots was to be expected; a steady drizzle had been haunting her for hours. The autumn rains had transformed the sandy ground into a sodden quagmire of wet leaves and mud that sucked at her soles and splattered all over her jeans.

The sky above was not any better. A somber blanket of gray clouds hid the sun and tempered what little optimism she was able to muster. She had reached the promised land of family and free rent. That should count for something. Just across the muddy yard was Aunt Randa's home, Baker Manor; a one-story colonial-style building of gray granite with a reddish-brown slate roof. It was a beautiful house, though a simple hedge and a few flower pots on the porch were the only visible attempts at landscaping. It was to be her home in the countryside for the foreseeable future, until she'd saved up enough for a house, or the down payment at least.

May took in the scene with a poorly veiled distaste, struggling to keep her sighs silent as her cousin Frank unloaded her boxes from the back of the truck.

"A little help here!" he called, staggering under the weight of her largest suitcase.

"Oh, sorry," May said, hurrying to lend him a hand. Not knowing what to expect from life in the countryside, and not particularly wanting to rent a storage unit, she had brought just about all of her possessions with her. It was heavy enough to shift the truck's alignment when driven, at least according to her cousin.

"So, where's Aunt Randa?" she asked. "I was expecting her at the airport,"

"She's out of town for a few days," Frank replied with a shrug, showcasing his broad shoulders, and bulging biceps while holding a bag almost as big as her. "Fundraising or some shit, I don't know. She has some meetings in the city and is apparently staying in a hotel in between."

They continued to drag boxes and bags from the trunk to the porch when they heard voices approaching upstairs. They looked up to see a skinny blonde girl in tight jeans and a rumpled white crop top. It was hard to miss her after she burst through the door of the balcony above them, shrieking with laughter. Her hair was a tangled mess and her eyes wild, but in a happy way.

Once those eyes caught sight of the truck, she stopped to stare.

A moment later, a young man with long, unkempt black hair followed her out, smiling softly and beginning to say something until he noticed what had caught her attention. May could not help but wonder how the cold air wasn't killing him, standing out in the rain shirtless. Maybe it was, maybe *that's* why he wrapped his arms around the girl and pulled her into his muscled torso. He even nuzzled his face hungrily into her neck.

"Hey Mary!" Frank called up from the yard. "Having fun?"

"Fraaank!" she called back, slightly slurred. "There's enough fun for everyone," she teased, though when her companion's huge hands came up to grope her breasts, she pulled away, still smiling as she playfully whacked him in the head.

"Come on, Ed, be nice. We got a guest to welcome, you horny bastard," Frank called back.

"I can see that," Mary observed with a nod toward May. "Who is this one? Can't say I've seen her before." She leaned forward for a closer look, swaying precariously over the front rail. Between her swaying and her broad smile, even a child could tell she was drunk.

"She's not one of *my* guests," Frank protested, turning to May who had stopped to watch the conversation, happy for an excuse to take a break from carrying the heavy bags. "She's just a cousin from the city, she's using the family's 'vast political connections' to get a job at the clinic," he said with a friendly blink in May's direction. He turned back to cast an accusing look at his brother. "And she would be settled already if my damn brother would come down from his castle and lend a hand! Seriously man, don't make me carry all this stuff myself."

Ed finally lifted his head, bypassing his brother to fix his gaze on May, his eyes steady and appraising. He looked for what seemed like a long time, his deep gray eyes scanning her from head to toe. It made her feel squeamish, and she struggled not to look away, blushing. Both of the twins shared a face, both *frustratingly* handsome with strong jaws.

Frank's looked rather grimy and rough. Ed's was smooth and clean shaven.

"Hello. . . cousin," he eventually said. His stare became somehow more intense with these words. She felt uneasy. "Welcome to the family," he said with a voice devoid of any emotion while squeezing his girl's breasts. It was enough to make May flinch. Anger, that was her first emotion, then indignation, and disgust at his vulgarity and to his blood cousin no less! It made her worry about just how far south she had traveled, and just how far he might take it. A sudden tingling feeling washed over her loins, staring up at that muscular, half-naked man as he shamelessly felt up his girlfriend right on the balcony for God and all else to see. Unable to bear the scuzzy tension any longer, she flushed a deep red and turned around, hurrying back to the truck for another bag.

"Come on, Mary, let's go meet my cousin," Ed said, finally heading inside and downstairs.

They met in the foyer as she dragged the last of her suitcases from the porch and out of the rain. Frank introduced them. "Ed, meet May, our cousin. May, meet Ed, the ugly twin, and his . . . um . . . Mary,"

"Hello, Frank's cousin" Mary slurred. May couldn't help but notice how out of place the massive bosom was compared to the rest of her small frame. "It's nice to meet you," she added. No move was made to shake hands or anything of the sort; she just stood smiling with those enormous front teeth. Combined with her plump, heavily freckled cheeks, she looked like a human-sized bunny dressed up in girls clothing.

May tried not to think of it; certainly she'd never *say* anything so horrible!

Ed was identical to his brother down to the cleft in their chins and slightly jagged noses. That is to say, again, he was *gorgeous*. Not less so with the dark, angry air he carried. It was such a contrast to how friendly and easygoing Frank had been since the moment he picked her up. Combined with the smoldering gray eyes, he was still making her tingly and wet, as shameful as that felt.

He was clearly ogling her, taking in the shape of her hips and chest.

"Hello, Ed," she said timidly, trying to ignore his look, "It's nice to meet you."

"The pleasure is all mine," he answered, starkly contrasting with the indifferent tone of his voice. The cold, detached face wasn't any more comforting, or any less attractive. It was a relief when he immediately walked away with his girl in tow, his hand drifting down to feel her butt.

She turned to Frank, looking confused. He only gave her a careless shrug and walked out of the room, dragging her suitcases behind him. The inside was markedly different from the yard. Furnished with artisan carved ebony, mahogany, and even ivory in some places. The cushions were soft and the den cozy, especially with the blazing fire in the hearth.

If she hadn't been so nervous, the sight might have made her smile. It was a beautiful house. After Frank helped get all her bags up to the bedroom she was borrowing and showed her the bathroom, suggesting a hot bath, she couldn't help but let out a faint smile. It sounded divine after all the rain she'd endured, and it was kind of him to let her go first, being just as wet and cold. The upstairs bathroom was no less beautiful or comfortable than the rest of the imposing house. The wide white tub submerged her, slowly making her aching limbs relax.

Dinner was simple, but delicious as well. A hearty soup with fresh homemade bread, and a pie for dessert to boot. It was better than what she had eaten in nursing college by a wide margin. It made her wonder where the food had even come from. She would have assumed Mary, in lack of a better alternative. She seriously doubted that her aunt spent any time on housework. Frank only half-heartedly tried to make conversation about university. It was just as well, she did not mind the lack of chatter. Ed appeared quite content with whatever he was doing under the table that made his drunk friend squee and blush during their meal. This was one of the stronger contributing factors to May's lack of motivation for polite conversing.

May ended up leaving before she was full, finishing her soup and taking a large piece of bread as she scampered out of the room. She nibbled thoughtfully on the bread while wandering through the house, looking at the odd, old ornaments here and there. A den that she had not passed through on the way in had an even larger hearth, almost as wide as it was long and with an expensive looking buffalo rug to boot.

She admired the dim, but beautiful room as she ate, not noticing until the bread was gone where she stood. The dark fur beneath her was covered in whitish bread crumbs, and it made her cringe immediately at the sort of impression she was cultivating, making such a mess. After a moment of thought, she called out, "Frank, where's the vacuum? I made a . . . small mess."

"Eh don't worry about it, Maggie'll clean it," his muffled voice called back from somewhere afar.

"Maggie?" May asked.

As if in response to the word, a slender woman appeared. She was older, May noted, in her early sixties by her estimate. She stood out from the others with her nut-brown skin and long gray hair. Also distinguishing herself from the rest by having her hair tightly bound in a work knot, not to mention the old-timey dress. Despite her slightly shriveled limbs and wrinkled features, she seemed to carry the vacuum without trouble, saying nothing, only smiling faintly as May stared. It just felt wrong to watch a woman nearly three-times her age clean up after her, but she couldn't think of anything to say.

"S-sorry about that, I wasn't thinking," she eventually stammered, earning a soft smile from the clearly seasoned woman. Despite her age, Maggie's eyes were clear and lucid. One of those gentle gazes that immediately put her at ease. "Did you bake that bread; it was delicious!" she praised, earning a low chuckle.

"Yes, I cook the meals here," she admitted, voice barely above a whisper, just a little strained even with her smile. "You're still standing on the rug, dear."

"Oh God, sorry, uh, let me get out of your way," May agreed, backing up a few steps. "It's a beautiful house, beautifully kept, I mean, uh . . . you do very good work!"

"Thank you. I take pride in my work, caring for the house, and those boys." It might have been her imagination, but May could swear her voice fell a bit further at the end of that sentence.

"Yeah they seem . . . Frank's real nice!" she was quick to point out. "You've known them a while?"

"I've worked here since *long* before they were born," she quipped, chuckling again at the widening of the new guest's eyes. "They're good kids, both of them. I know Ed is cold and . . . angry, he-he's been dealing with some difficult times lately, but you don't have to worry about him. He would never hurt you," she assured, reading the young woman's mind. At least that was May's initial thought. More likely she'd overheard some of their conversing from wherever she was.

"Well . . . thank you, i-it's a little frightening, being so far from home with two strange men."

"Of course; now you should get some rest, find something better to do then watch an old crone work at least," she insisted, flooding the room with the noisy vacuum, just in case May didn't get the hint. She did. She walked away from the conversation with a smile, relieved for the new information and the new acquaintance.

Now full, warm, and far less stressed, she headed for bed.

The utter contentment she had lying down between the slightly stiff, pressed sheets was soured quickly. The sounds of Mary's shuddering moans drifting in from the room across the hallway brought the discomfort back tenfold. It was too late to crank the volume on anything, and her books were not distracting enough to drown out the guttural sounds of pleasure.

It was hours before she slept.

CHAPTER 2

The sun was just barely in the sky and already May was on her way to work. The dim morning air formed a thick mist as the black Ford lurched and wobbled down the rough dirt road leading to the county's only clinic. May sat quietly for most of the ride, her nerves plain on her face as she clutched tightly to her seatbelt, trying not to feel the jolts to her spine each time the car jerked from the potholes in the road Aunt Randa did not seem to notice.

Her eyes remained fixed ahead on the road with an irritated look, her face pristine only because of the caked-on makeup hiding her wrinkles. The view of her shriveled hands on the steering wheel made that all too clear.

She had been back in town for three days, and all she talked about was the ongoing congressional election; that or all the things that needed fixing in Springdale. She had barely even greeted May. At the present moment, the poor road conditions were the subject so much more important than her beginning her first day of a completely new job in a completely unfamiliar town.

"Can you see the condition of this road?" she complained. "The lumberjacks and their big trucks come all the way from Wood's End, fell our trees, wreck our roads, and don't pay a single red cent to the local council for reconstruction!" She turned to May, words sharp. "Do you think that's fair, dear?"

"No," she offered cautiously, not quite expecting to be dragged into the monologue. "No ma'am, it's not," she managed, lapsing back into her nervous silence. She stared out the window at the gray, somber sky, a fair reflection of her own melancholic mood. She already hated this town, with its gloomy skies and cold, wet air. The way every inch of earth was either wet grass, a muddy road, or a farm field made her skin crawl. The sheer emptiness of the countryside unnerved her. Not least of all, the forest, a primeval woodland of giant oaks, birches, firs, and a hundred other species of trees she couldn't name. They stretched to the right of the road as far as the eyes could see.

It made her hope for *more* lumberjacks to drive on in, not that she could ever voice that thought.

Aunt Randa nodded in agreement, seeming to barely hear her niece as she launched back into her tirade. "Mark this," she said with a stony determination etched on her face. "My first act as mayor would be to reinstate the wood taxes from the Union era. These men need to pay the due price for selling *our* county's timber!"

"How about dress taxes first, for people who intentionally dress like a cliché hillbilly?" Frank suggested from the back of the car. He leaned upward, getting uncomfortably close as he continued. "Really, May, overalls? You're not making fun of us inbred country bumpkins, are ya?"

"Language, Frank," Aunt Randa chided. "Though he's not wrong, dear," she said looking over May's choice of clothes. "I know this is the countryside and all, but people don't dress like this anymore. Don't you have any of those fancy clothes you big city people usually wear?"

May looked herself over. She wore a maroon-colored shirt and a thick pair of overalls over it. She had dressed trying to fit in, and that made the critiques hurt all the more. Maggie dressed old-timey like!

"This is the way I always dress, ma'am," she lied weakly. "It's comfortable."

"I know, dear," said Aunt Randa in her usual *nice-aunty* voice. "It's just that it's unusual; it'll get people talking about you and our family, and I *really* don't need that right now with the election so close," she explained, softening the slightest bit as May slouched in on herself. "I mean, surely the boys would be more responsive if you dressed prettier?"

The remark made her squeamish, and she sank into herself yet further, feeling even more miserable.

"Maybe she doesn't like boys," Frank defended. "Maybe she's more of a soft butch."

"Oh shut up, Frank!" Aunt Randa snapped, turning to May with a grim look in her eyes. "You do like boys, right?"

She nodded timidly.

"Yeah . . . It's just—

"Oh, good . . . glad to hear that, dear," her aunt announced merrily while cutting her off. "We'll fix you up yet, turn you into a *proper* young lady. Then they'll be eating out of your hand."

They drove in blessed silence for a while after that remark, passing farms, ranches, and even an apple orchard before they pulled into the Maria Claire's Memorial Clinic. A simple two-story building of whitewashed sandstone with a marble statue of a praying woman that could only be Saint Maria, kneeling over a water fountain at the front. The giant stone woman was more than a little eerie-looking in the stifling fog.

May gave a polite farewell to her aunt and cousin before heading in the front door, clutching tightly to her various forms and orientation papers.

She had arrived early, and that left her unsure how to react to the empty reception counter. Her shoes echoed off the marble floors as she made her way down and around the steps. Halfway down, she spotted a sign that read *nurse's hold* above the door. That room was empty, too, except for a lone woman sitting at the counter with her head on the desk. Approaching the counter slowly, and clearing her throat seemed to get her attention.

"Hello?"

The sleepy nurse looked up with red, tired eyes, blinking at her through tousled blonde hair.

"Well, you're not Aaron."

"Uh, yeah, I know," May replied lamely. She couldn't help but wonder, *why is everyone so goddamn strange in this place?* Did she not have a boss that would fire her or at least chew her out for sleeping on the job?

"And you're not Joseph, the coffee guy." May checked to make sure she was, in fact, a girl before replying.

"No, no, I am not the coffee guy," she returned, daring to sound a little annoyed.

"Yeah, you're prettier by far. So then, who are you?"

May took a deep breath, trying not to let her frustration show.

"I'm May Staunton, the new counter nurse. I was told I'd be starting today," she explained, annoyed and uncomfortable as she stared at an extremely interesting exit sign above her. There were few things she found more annoying than drawing on a conversation for no reason.

"Oh, that's you?" said the woman while inspecting her closely. "I thought we were getting someone . . . younger,"

"Well, it's me," May said, fidgeting with a thread that had loosened in the seam of her overalls.

"Cool, I'm Dana," she replied with a smirk. "My friends call me Dana, at least. Welcome to MCMC!" she offered, finally sounding awake as she extended a pale, slim hand.

May reached to shake it but was interrupted by a second figure. A dark-haired young man with a long, messy beard rose from behind the counter rubbing his head. Seeing that he was naked except for a pair of tight underpants with a conspicuous bulge at the crotch froze May up. She even stumbled back a few steps.

Dana groaned in annoyance of her own, turning her eyes back to the man.

"What are you still doing here?" she demanded, stealing a glance at her watch. "It's almost six-thirty!"

"Wha . . . what?" he stammered, still groggy from sleep. "Where are my clothes?"

"I don't fucking know; what am I, your mom?" she snapped at him. "Just find them and get out before the doctors arrive; you weren't even supposed to sleep here!"

May stood aside, watching the whole exchange in mild shock, trying not to stare at the duo as they searched the room. Despite her words, Dana helped him search. May couldn't bring herself to lend a hand in the searching efforts. It took her full attention not to steal glances at the naked man. He was handsome, in a dad-bod sort of way. His mussed hair and muscled pecs gave a rough edge of beauty, and to her horror, his bulging crotch hanging heavily between his legs kept calling out to her out of the corner of her vision. She was mortified when he caught her staring and flashed a wicked smile back. Blood filled her face, and she turned away yet further to stare at the blank wall.

Thankfully, two minutes later, give or take, Dana's companion was fully clothed and walking out the office door. A laugh rang out at something she couldn't hear as his huge hand wrapped around the nurse's slender waist and then down to grab her butt. The distinct smack of a kiss was the last thing May heard before she strolled back in.

"Sorry you had to see that," Dana said, though her tone was anything but remorseful. "In my defense, nothing ever happens during the night shifts, so sometimes a lady craves a little entertainment."

"I guess that's about the only entertainment there is out here," May replied dryly. "So that was like . . . your boyfriend?"

The other girl laughed like if it was the funniest thing she had ever heard.

"Boyfriend?" she echoed. "Tony's way too much of a slob, *but* he gives really good oral, among other things, and that makes him tolerable," she explained. "Definitely not a boyfriend though. Come along now, I'll show you where to change," she finished, happy to change the subject as she led her back into the locker room.

CHAPTER 3

It was a few minutes past one, near the end of her shift, when Dana strolled back to the counter where May sat. The senior employee smiled sympathetically as her new coworker looked up; she couldn't help it. The poor girl looked lost in the pile of papers on the desk, more than a little stressed, too.

After a little rest and a good wash, Dana looked refreshed; more than that, she looked ten years younger. The long-legged, twenty-two-year-old woman casually rested her elbows on the desk, looking down with clear blue eyes bordered by impossibly long, curved lashes.

With a slender nose, prominent cheekbones, and full pink lips, she was one of the most beautiful women May had ever seen. Her long platinum hair was brushed back and bound by a pale blue ribbon that matched both her eyes the sapphire stone hanging from a chain around her neck.

She continued staring down at May, smiling pleasantly as she spoke.

"How are you holding up?"

"I'm alright," May replied, grateful for the concern. "It's a lot but . . . everyone here seems nice, and the doctors are being patient with me."

"They better be; don't forget, it's *damn* hard to convince a nurse to move all the way out here, not to mention working for this crap pay. They need you more than you need them," she assured. "Just smile at the patients, get their names, mark them for appointments, and that's ninety percent of the job. A great job for a pretty face and an empty head."

May nodded slowly, not quite sure how to reply.

"Oh, I meant for *me*, to be clear, that's why the job is so great for me," she quickly explained. "Earlier today," said Dana, breaking the silence when May didn't. "You seemed pretty disturbed by all that, with Tony. I wanted to apologize. Have you never seen a guy naked before?" She had a look in her eyes that May had seen all too often, the one that surfaced whenever the boys at her school teased her or made vulgar remarks about her.

"No," she admitted sheepishly.

"Well, you might as well get used to it, it is part of being a nurse here," she explained. "Though the ones coming in asking *you* to get naked, just curse them out, or flirt with them if they're cute, your choice. Just keep in mind, it's all a part of the job. People out here in the countryside tend to be a bit too honest and . . . unrefined. A pretty face and a . . . *calm* head, remember?" Dana had just finished her advice when the main door opened and a young man in a dark green jacket, brown pants, and red beanie walked into the reception, coming straight for the counter. Seeing him, Dana decided to give the newbie a bit more. "Oh my God, May," Dana whispered. "Watch out for this creep. He's gotta be a rapist or a serial killer or something, he lives out alone in the woods."

"What?" May protested. "I can't talk to him!"

"Too late. Smile," Dana suggested, quickly slipping away from reception and back to the nurses hold, leaving May alone with the stranger.

"Good morning. Welcome to MCMC," she recited from the lines she had memorized. "Do you have an appointment?"

"Yeah, yes, I have an appointment with Doctor Stan in DNA processing, but I think I'm a bit early. Is he in?" he asked softly, *abnormally* softly, and so quiet that she struggled to hear him.

"No, he hasn't signed in yet," May replied after checking her book. "Would you like to wait for him; it shouldn't be more than a few minutes."

"No problem," he replied, unnerving her by not leaving the counter. He was examining her closely and she knew what he saw. The same image she saw every morning in the mirror, a pear-shaped face with raven-colored hair, adorned with one streak of silver, painfully innocent eyes of vivid green framed with thin, meager lashes. Her worst feature, the pug nose, sat just above a pair of narrow lips.

This girl had a pleasant face perfect for shy smiles, the man thought, the nervous grin she held currently was pretty adorable, too. Not less so with the cute pink blush faint on her cheeks. Still, he noticed he was making her uncomfortable with the staring, he had to stop.

"So uh . . . do you like flowers?" he asked abruptly, trying to break the silence.

"Yes, I uh, suppose," she replied, trying to be polite.

"What's your favorite flower?" he asked, drawing her eyes back to his own hazel ones. The gaze looked innocent enough, even if the question was treading into uncertain waters. Still, she answered.

"White tulips."

"Oh, that suits you," he offered.

"Excuse me?"

"Well, you . . . sort of have an innocent vibe; white symbolizes innocence, right?" he asked. "If you go on a date with me, I'll bring you some," he offered bluntly.

Rapist . . . Serial killer, Dana's voice echoed in her head.

"You think I'm that easy to woo over?" she joked back, as if she hadn't considered his offer for a second.

"Okay, wrong move," he said, maybe to himself. "Can I try again from the start?"

"I would rather we jump straight to the end," she mocked, trying to sound more confident and nonchalant than she actually was. Trying her damndest to follow Dana's advice.

"Well, that would involve things that are best left for private eyes," he teased with a playful smile. "You know, if it ends the way I'm hoping,"

"Has anyone ever told you that you're an overly confident man?" May teased.

"Someone just did," he replied, gazing into her eyes. "Believe it or not, I don't talk to girls often." May was forced to smile. He had a way with words; there was no denying it. He seemed gentle and smart, direct but not *too* inappropriate in his approach. "I'm Samuel . . . as you already know from your book," he said, coughing and extending his hand. "But I'd like you to call me Sam."

She tried taking the compliment while keeping calm, cool, and collected, despite herself.

"May," she replied, taking his offered greeting, and not even pulling back when he squeezed her hand softly.

"So, May, you're new here, aren't you?" he observed. "I feel like I would have noticed you," he said, making her stomach flutter. As she continued the silent appraisal, she couldn't deny that he was handsome. Also, this was far more male attention then she was used to. Under his red beanie was a mop of heavy chestnut hair that fell down below his ears. His stare was intense and unflinching, eyes that seemed to see much but give away little. But his smile was warm, and the soft tone he spoke with did much to ease the tension around them. Suffice to say, she turned a deep shade of pink before answering.

"Yes, I am. I got into town last week."

"Then permit me to welcome you to Springdale." He spread his arms in mock introduction. "It's the only town with the word 'spring' attached that feels like winter half the year."

They both laughed. He had a good laugh, a deep tenor with a musical ring. She couldn't help but judge Dana for what she said about him, even if that tidbit about where he lived was true. There was something odd about him, but he didn't seem dangerous.

"So, I know a spot in the woods where wild white tulips grow, the best flowers you can find anywhere in the region. Would you like to come on a walk with me out there? Maybe grab a meal afterwards or something?"

"Is that another attempt at a date?" She cocked her head at him, trying to sound enticing in that way she'd seen on more confident girls.

"Would you still come if it was?"

"Oh, I think I would," she admitted; it was an enticing offer after all. "Only for the tulips, mind you."

He gave her a broad grin again, bright-eyed with amusement.

"Of course, why else would you come?"

It was then the doctor strolled in and their conversation ended. She only got a quick wave and confirmation of pickup time on his way out after the appointment, managing to keep dignified for both and even offering a flirty wave as he slipped out the door.

Inside she was squealing like a schoolgirl who had just been asked to her first dance.

CHAPTER 4

It was late afternoon when May found the grove. It laid hidden behind a huge blackberry bush at the point where the stream curved around a large rock; easy to find by following the water. It was a bit frightening, trekking her way through the thick forest to the remote parts off the trails. Maybe even stupid of her, though she had told both Dana and Frank where she was going. She also told them when she should be back, who she was with, and she made sure any potential serial killers knew that she had done so.

Dana had seemed horrified when May told her about her date in the woods. She had even begged her not to go, worried he would rape, murder, and bury her in an unmarked grave beside the stream. May had stubbornly refused, insisting she was tired of people warning her about the danger of boys while having all the fun themselves. Everyone in this fucking town seemed horny to a fault so far; she would be damned if she was going to miss out.

So, here she was, standing in the middle of the forest with a flower basket in hand, waiting for a strange man she had just met earlier that day. Nothing about it seemed remotely sensible. She wasn't even planning to live down here long-term.

May took a breath and forced herself to relax. It was a clear, sunny day with hardly a cloud in sight. The sun sent down shafts of bright golden rays, breaching the foliage overhead in a dozen shades of green, brown, and gold. The air was cool under the treetops, almost pleasant. The smell of wet earth, dead leaves, and rotting fruits was also surprisingly pleasant, not offensive, in any case. Birds chirped from their nests while darting from one tree to the other on speedy wings every which way.

She felt small.

"Sam!" she called, her voice rolling down between the trees. Birds burst into flight from the sudden noise, and she craned her head to look around, searching for any sign of her date. Though his voice was heard long before she got eyes on him.

"Over here!" he cried.

Startled by his proximity, she crested a small hill to find him leaning casually on a tree. His eyes ran slowly down the length of her frame with a faint look of fascination. She could tell that he liked what he saw, even before he confirmed it.

"You look beautiful."

"Oh, thank you," she mumbled, blushing immediately. She had changed from her 'hillbilly' clothes into a sleeveless crop top, a knee-high pleated skirt, and flat shoes.

"I couldn't come out wearing nothing," she added, trying to sound spicy, "So, I wore the next best thing."

"I like it," he replied with a casual smile. "Never unwrap the present until Christmas, right?"

She wondered what he meant by that but chose to remain ignorant out of fear of looking stupid.

"You look good, too," she offered. He had discarded his 'serial killer' outfit for a red sweater and brown trousers, but he still sported the same red beanie and old work boots. She envied the latter as they walked close to the river, where the mud seeped up into her socks. She had hesitated for a moment there, that, of all things, making her wonder if she should go.

"Are you coming or what? The flowers are this way."

With a deep breath, she continued on. She caught up quickly, trailing behind with her small basket loaded with fruits, cheese, and sandwiches; he hadn't commented on it. For the life of her, she couldn't think of how to bring up the dinner she had brought without sounding like some silly little girl. They walked silently for a while, though the soft murmuring of the stream beside them made for a pleasant white noise.

"So, are you from around here?" she asked.

"Around here?" he asked, surveying the nearby trees. "This forest, you mean?"

"No, not the forest," she said with a chuckle. "I meant Springdale. Are you from here?"

"I'm from Westbrook; it's just a few hours from here."

"Westbrook?" she asked, furrowing her brow in pensive thought. "Can't say I've heard of it."

"You haven't," he assured with an air of dismissal. "It's a small town a few miles south of here, just across the woods. Even smaller then Springdale, there's not much to say about it."

"So, did you have any girlfriends over there?" she teased, immediately regretting it, nervous about his response.

"I had a few brief dallies with the town girls, nuthin' special."

"What were they like?" she inquired. "Those *town* girls?"

"They were the same as anyone, I would guess," he said, not sure what else she wanted, but amused by her curiosity. "They all had two eyes, two ears, two hands, two legs . . . and two pairs of lips. As I said, nothing special."

"They had two pairs of lips?" she asked innocently. There was something about the way he said it that left her suspecting a more implied meaning to the statement. Then the humiliation hit her like a mallet.

"Yes, they did," he offered, delighting in that blush. "But never mind that."

"Did you . . . kiss them often?" she asked anxiously, a good while later. "I mean, on both pairs of lips?" she asked, awkwardly attempting to joke away her previous ignorance. But she could not deny that it also was an attempt at trying to bring back the lewd conversation.

He laughed at that.

"In public, just one," he explained. "In private though . . . well a gentleman never tells, right? Why do you ask?" He looked sideways at her, studying her face with a hint of amusement in his eyes.

"No reason," she lied, struggling to fight the color rising to her cheeks.

"Have you ever been kissed? On either pair?"

She laughed nervously, trying to hide her obvious unease.

"Not really. My dad didn't allow me to be around boys." It was the same story she told everyone who cared enough to ask, but the truth was almost the exact opposite. That she was too embarrassed by her drunk of a father to have anyone close. This, compounded with her missing mother, left her unsure how to interact with boys as she grew up, even if she wanted to.

"Wow, that's sad," he offered. "I'm sure he had his reasons."

"I guess," she replied tersely, before wriggling her hands playfully. "Can I tell you a secret?"

"Of course. My lips are sealed," he offered. Though despite his assuring smile, she took a deep breath to calm her nerves.

"I'll be twenty-two in a few months. That's over two decades, and I know I'm not *that* bad looking. Still, I've never been on a date, until now." She felt like a sulky little child complaining to him about it, but she couldn't stop. "I've never had a boyfriend. My dad was both my date and chaperone at my prom. I've never even been kissed before."

He was silently still for a while after hearing that. From the look on his face, she couldn't tell what he was thinking. Though a part of her was sure that he thought her a weirdo. She grew yet more certain of that fact with each passing second, and desperately, she tried to think of an apology when he finally spoke.

"Well, I'm honored," he said lightly, almost like a joke. The relief of those words crashed over her like a wave. "Would you like to be kissed?" he asked in a barely audible whisper. In an instant, the tension was back.

"Right now, here?" she asked, feeling strangely uncertain. "I-I don't know . . ."

"I do," he whispered, leaning in to kiss her gently on the lips.

She just stared, her eyes wide-open, grasping the situation. He took her hand in his, sending tiny tingles up her arms. He held the kiss for a few moments before pulling away, leaving her completely flustered and frowning heavily.

"Shit, sorry, I shouldn't have done that," he apologized, clearly embarrassed by her reaction. "I'm sorry. I thought you wanted to."

"No, I did," she explained. "I just . . . wasn't ready,"

"I'm sorry," he repeated.

"Over there," she said, pointing to an extensive glade across the stream.

It was a roughly semicircular shape, at least twenty feet across at its widest part and bordered by the stream bed on one side. Gold-leafed rowan trees followed along the opposite side of the water in a breathtaking display. The treetops were open to the sky, allowing sunlight to cascade over a bed of ankle-length grass. Still, despite all there was to see, May was most mesmerized by the dozen varieties of flowers. She had never seen anything more beautiful, white tulips, yellow sunflowers, purple orchids, yellow dandelions, red, white, and even rare black roses. All wildly jumbled in a burst of colors and pageantry that, for a moment, she couldn't quite believe was really there. The clear waters of the stream sparkled in the late afternoon as the sun cast an otherworldly collage of shadows.

Nowhere could she have imagined such beauty in the middle of this dreary woodland realm.

"Come on," he said, bending down to unlace his boots. "Take off your shoes. We're going across," he took off his boots and cuffed his trousers while she slipped off her own simple tennis shoes.

With her hand in his, she slowly climbed down into the stream. She shivered slightly as the ice-cold water hit her feet. They moved slowly, checking for footing as they waded knee-deep across the muddy stream bed before emerging on the other side.

Mud squished between her toes while blades of grass tickled her ankles. The ground was warm, and the air smelled sweeter than she had ever known. Sam stepped beside her wiggling his toes and flapping his legs, spraying water everywhere.

"Stop that!" she shouted, stumbling to get away from his playful aquatic attack. "You're going to get me wet."

"So easily?" he laughed, moving closer again with soaked trousers. "I would have expected it'd take more than just soaked trousers to get a fox like you wet."

She shook her head, chuckling.

"You, sir, have a really dirty mind, do you know that?"

Thank you," he replied. "But enough of that, let's get started. These tulips aren't gonna pick themselves."

He laid off the dirty talk from there. They spent the rest of the afternoon picking flowers, lazing under the sun, and sharing an early dinner of cucumber sandwiches and other goodies she had packed. Butterflies fluttered around them in a colorful parade while they ate.

The sun was setting as he some time later walked May home. She carried two bouquets of flowers in her basket *and* a beautiful flower garland on her head that Sam had made her.

At the crossroads beside the old abandoned town hall, he stopped to check his watch and peer up at the sky.

"I have to turn back now. It's getting late, and I really want to sell some flowers before the day's up."

"You sell them?"

"Yeah, by the intersection up east out of town; it's kept me fed so far."

"Do you have to go right now though?" She pouted. "Can't you at least finish walking me home?"

"No, I really can't." He stopped and took her hands in his, looking genuinely apologetic. "This won't be the last time we meet, I promise,"

"Alright," she reluctantly agreed. "Thank you for the flowers. I had the most wonderful time."

"Me too," he said. "Let's do this again."

"You know where to find me. Goodnight, Sam."

"Goodnight, May."

And as the last light of the sun vanished beyond the western horizon, they each went their separate ways. A pale, crescent moon was beginning to shine in the sky. May couldn't ever remember being so giddy.

***

As she approached the house, May heard loud voices.

Angry voices.

Aunt Randa's Explorer was parked in the driveway beside Ed's navy blue car. Frank's truck was nowhere to be seen. Most likely it was parked at the *clubhouse*, a glorified strip club where he fucked his whores and drank himself stupid. At least that was how her aunt described what took place inside those walls, and the first and only time May had asked about his absence.

As she stepped onto the patio, she heard the voice clearly. The shrill sound of her furious aunt, bickering with the softer, low, and yet icy tone of her youngest son. After about a week at Baker Manor, she came to understand Frank a little bit. The older twin was loud and extremely uncouth, but always helpful and easygoing. Crueler folks might call him a lecher, or even a drunk; although he seemed utterly unashamed of his vices. Always making those vulgar jokes and telling his stories. Still, he seemed harmless enough. She appreciated his jovial takes and dark humor, it eased the otherwise rather depressive and gloomy atmosphere in the house.

The younger twin remained an enigma. He never talked much; he moved around the house like a pariah, kept his head down, and only answered questions in as few words as possible. She'd never seen him drunk, or drink any alcohol even. He barely seemed to eat. His dark, gray eyes showed only two emotions: anger and lust, the former of which always seemed directed at her. Very often he would stare at her coldly, anger simmering behind his narrow eyes. What unnerved her the most, though, was just how similar those eyes were to the way he looked at his lover. How it seemed in any instant, he might switch from fury to an intense look of absolute lust, grab her and do who knows what. It made her desperately nervous most of the time. Sure, they were cousins, but this *was* the country, and rape happened within the family often. Or so she had heard the rumors go. She got more comfort from the fact he never made any advances or sought out other girls; his focus seemed safely locked on Mary, his buxom, freckled girlfriend.

May slowly edged the door open and snuck into the house, walking softly on her toes. She had no intention of being dragged into their latest debacle. Her aunt's voice drifting down from the lobby upstairs gave her the gist of it. She was complaining about something. She was always complaining about something, whether it was the rising cost of heating their house, the number of stupid kids embracing the LGBT movement, or the fact that church attendance was dwindling before her eyes. It always seemed to start out of the blue, first a gently expressed thought and soon, an angry rambling scolding toward anyone who happened to walk by her.

Tonight, the oral assault was directed at her youngest son.

"This is still my house, you hear me?" she screeched, "and I will be damned if I sit by while you turn it into your whorehouse!" A loud banging upstairs made her flinch. "I've endured your brother's shit, coming home late, drunk out of his mind; I will NOT sit around while you bring your whores into my house!"

"Don't call her that," Ed repeated, low and seething with anger. "Mary is not a whore."

"Don't use that tone with me, boy!" she growled. "I'm still your mother, and I can call her whatever the hell I please. This is MY house!"

"Fuck this," May heard him say. The sound of boots on the stairs and a slamming door made clear that he was leaving. As if she could blame him.

"Of course!" Aunt Randa called after him. "You're gonna walk out on your mother. Go on then, walk away, just like your worthless father."

May watched him through the front window as he slammed the door of his car, speeding away from the house and down the road. In the efforts of stealth, she waited a few minutes before creeping up the stairs to her room. Outside the master bedroom, she heard her aunt's muffled sobs punctuated by sudden distressing squeals. May rolled her eyes, not pausing until she realized her aunt was on the phone.

"No Matt, I can't take it anymore. These boys are driving me crazy; they don't appreciate anything I do for them. I can't . . ." A pause. "No, I can handle Frank; it's Edward I'm worried about." May knew she should not eavesdrop, but she couldn't help herself. She leaned in closer, pressing her ear toward the door so as not to be discovered.

"Him?" her Aunt Randa asked after a long pause. "He left the house . . . He's so angry, Matt . . . He hates me; I can see it in his eyes. My own son hates me!" She broke into another bout of body-shuddering sobs. "I don't know what to do. He needs to know, Matt. He needs to know the truth." Suddenly, May heard quick footsteps approaching the door, and darted off down the dark hall into her room, closing the door behind her.

She could only wonder at the conversation she just heard. *"He needs to know the truth,"* her aunt had said. *What truth was that? Was that the boys' father, maybe?* It was rumored that some businessman-turned-senator had gotten her pregnant when she was a girl and skipped town. It's where Aunt Randa got the house, a house she was left to raise the boys *all alone* in, as she bemoaned. As if Maggie didn't do all the laundry, cooking, cleaning, and all the other grunt work for her. It occurred to May there were more secrets behind these dreary gray walls than she thought. Secrets about her aunt and her strange sons, secrets that might shatter the fragile peace of her new home.

May prepared for bed, thinking of what she could possibly do as she reflected over her first day of work. It had begun with a cold, gloomy morning, an utterly *wonderful* afternoon, and was now a downward spiral of doubts, clandestine calls, and whispered secrets.

She tossed and turned, fearing where this all might lead.

CHAPTER 5

May sat at the front desk of the clinic, staring at the open pages of the appointment book. Her mind was elsewhere—two miles away in the middle of the woods, to be exact. She remembered the beautiful glade where they picked flowers, the way the butterflies had seemed to float around her date.

Daydreaming about yesterday was a pleasant way to pass her shift. She imagined looking up and seeing him walking toward her desk, clutching a white tulip as an invitation for another date.

Her day in the woods had been most enjoyable, even crossing the cold, icy stream with bare feet! She loved watching the sunset over the woods while standing on the cool earth, toes in the mud. She wanted to go again, she wanted that feeling of being free and alive.

May was so lost in thought, she didn't notice Dana sneaking up from behind her.

"Penny for your thoughts?" she asked, snapping May back into reality with a sharp jump. "Quit daydreaming, girl. Are you thinking about your serial killer again?"

"Don't call him that," May protested. "He's a really cool guy, and he treats me nice."

"You sound smitten, girl," Dana teased. "Are you in love with him already?"

"Of course not!" she denied. "We're just hanging out, you know . . . having fun."

"Having fun? How much fun exactly have you had?" Dana asked, smiling mischievously. "I know it takes more than flowers to please a woman."

"No, we haven't done anything like that," May replied, feeling the heat rising to her cheeks. "Well, he kissed me once, but . . ."

"But what?" Dana asked. "You didn't turn him down, did you?"

"I wasn't ready, you know," she protested weakly. "My dad never let me have a boyfriend or even be around guys. I've never done it before, and I didn't want to rush." She didn't like Dana asking about Sam. She wasn't sure how she felt about him yet. He was handsome in a boyish kind of way, and smart, fun to talk to. Also, despite his vulgar remarks from time to time, he didn't seem to be in any hurry to get into her pants.

She appreciated that.

She didn't want to rush into something she wasn't prepared for. Though she didn't want to seem like some love-struck teenage girl who just had her first kiss either. May had resolved to play it cool; she even shook her hair saucily with her next words, "If a boy wants my attention, he better work to earn it," she declared.

"That's too bad," Dana replied, with a light laugh. "I already called Tony over for the night shift. If you wanted, he could show you a few things about being a woman."

"Oh my god, absolutely not" May replied, disgusted but with her heart suddenly racing. "Tony's too rough and unkempt. Besides, I've seen him before, he's just . . . way too big." She still blushed whenever she remembered the look he had given her, just after he caught her looking at his crotch. He seemed like the kind of guy who never drew lines about what he would do with a woman, never considering how far a woman was willing to go or not before he stopped. Even if he was handsome, even if a slight tingling ache pulsated in her loins when remembering him half naked, she was not comfortable around him.

"That's precisely what you want in your man, dear," Dana assured, laughing in that naughty way she always did. "You'll understand it in due time."

"Well, I'll stick with Sam, thank you," she added. Dana snorted in amusement. It sounded childish to her, but Dana didn't give her coworker any more shit about it for the rest of the shift. May seemed really excited.

* * *

The queue at the ticket stand stretched for half a block, with moviegoers nervously watching the dark clouds that promised an evening of heavy rain, all hoping to get inside before it started. Sam gazed sullenly at the slow-moving line while everyone desperately waited for admission to the new romantic thriller that was making waves across the nation. He wanted to be elsewhere, *anywhere* but here, but May wanted a real date. Apparently, in the big city, *real* couples went on dates at the cinema.

After thirty minutes on a bus and almost two miles of walking from their starting point, they finally found one of these mystical movie theaters. He just hoped to hell she enjoyed it. The short hike especially made him worry that this was a d-rank date at best.

She was really suffering, too, he noticed, sweltering in the extreme, muggy heat. May had dressed as lightly as possible in her sleeveless white silk top, with a set of jean shorts, and simple sandals to match. Sweat beads gathered around her face and ran down her neck, absorbed into her clothes by the time they reached the line. He couldn't help but stare, her breasts damp as the sweat-soaked blouse clung to them, revealing how perfectly shaped they were, how *large*. Not to mention her long, black hair draped attractively across her shoulders in a braid. He'd never seen her so sexy.

"What?" she asked, noticing his gaze.

"Nothing," he replied a bit too quickly. "I was only staring . . . at something I never thought I'd ever see."

"And what's that?" she asked, raising a brow and placing a hand on her hips.

"Someone hotter than this blasted sun?" he tried. May tried not to smile, but she failed. With that line broken, she quickly fell into a short laugh of disbelief.

"Really?" she asked, still grinning ear to ear. "Did you write that one down? I wonder how long you spent coming up with that."

"I never need to write anything down. I'm barely literate!" he claimed staunchly, earning another laugh. "You're a steady source of inspiration."

"And you're a steady source of cheesy jokes, aren't you?"

"I always aim to please, madame," he said with a phony French accent; May laughed again.

They shuffled their way up to the ticket counter, finally getting their tickets, popcorn, and drinks without any further teasing. The half derelict little theater felt surprisingly cozy with

Sam next to her. Still, they sat in the back row, in the center where they had a view of the entire theater.

The movie began, and within a few minutes, Sam grew bored. Not that this was a surprise to him. He ate his popcorn and moved on to stealing May's when he noticed her intense focus on what was unravelling on the screen. May seemed utterly enraptured by the story, her eyes glistening with tears at the cheesy fight scene he'd lost track of.

Sam watched her cry in morbid curiosity; her pain was, in fact, real, he could tell. It broke his heart to see her cry. That was what spurred him to stretch his hand across her seat and wrap his arm around her shoulder to pull her close. She placed her head on his shoulder without a word. Her soft hair tickled his face as gentle tears escaped her eyes and rolled down her cheeks.

His heart rate accelerated, and all he could think of was how to push things. About pulling her gaze up to him, comforting her with a smile and maybe stealing another kiss. An overwhelming urge to hold and protect her from harm grew in him. Though that just made him think of sourer subjects, of the truth he was hiding from her, and how much he wanted to share it. Maybe she would understand, maybe she wouldn't care.

There was only one way to find out.

He resolved then that he would tell her after the movie, maybe on the ride home. But fate had it's own plans. By the time they left the theater, the sun had retreated behind a thick veil of ominous dark clouds. The wind blew with an ever-increasing strength, and whatever angry god oversaw the rains today began stirring up a stormy cauldron.

They made a mad dash for the bus station. The storm hit, lashing angrily at man, beast, and vehicle alike, rain falling sideways in its intensity. Ten minutes later, they finally huddled together in the back of the bus, drenched to the bone, and shivering with cold, his confession long forgotten.

* * *

It was eight P.M. when May returned to the clinic for the night shift; Frank had been kind enough to drop her off with his truck. Despite this kindness, she escaped quickly out the passenger side, desperate to find fresh air. Her chauffeur reeked of alcohol, stale sweat, and vomit. He barely reacted to the soft thanks she offered before sprinting inside.

It had rained all day, and now, the night air was cool and wet, though dark clouds still covered the moon and stars, threatening her with another shower. As she walked up to the doors, she pulled the collar of her coat tighter around her neck. Last time she saw her, Dana had claimed she would have an exciting surprise for her waiting at work. Though May could hardly imagine anything that would be more exciting than the adventure she had with Sam.

They had taken the bus home, huddled together in the back seats for warmth like they were trying to survive a blizzard. Her wet skin pressed against his as the rain lashed at the windows. Rain that raged and shoved their heavy bus all the way back to Springdale. There, they were stuck in a crowd of equally stranded commuters. It was almost sundown before the rain had stopped enough for people to leave. He'd been so quiet for the ride, but his smile was reassuring. Which made it all the more surprising that when she had abruptly hugged him before running off, she felt his erection pressed hard against her thigh.

She was embarrassed in the moment, but now, looking back on it, it made her excited. Proud even, in some strange way; knowing that he thought about her that way. That maybe he was even thinking about her right now, alone, doing something naughty. May was nearing the main entrance when she spotted Tony in the driveway, leaning on his pickup and finishing a massive cigar. He was dressed in a tight-fit olive T-shirt that emphasized his wide shoulders, and a simple pair of jeans. His mussed hair and now close-cropped beard gave him a roughhewn sexual appeal that looked dangerous, thrilling.

He noticed her staring. Worse, he leered right back, raising a brow as he slowly placed a hand on his crotch and gave it a gentle shake. She blushed, quickly averting her eyes as she fled into the clinic, terrified of drawing his attention more then she already had. It was only more nerve-wracking now that she had to worry about Sam's reaction as well.

Inside, the building was almost deserted. Most of the staff were gone for the day, leaving only a minimal crew to stand guard for emergencies and run the overnight duties. She found Dana at the nurse's counter, staring furtively at her watch.

"May, where have you been?" she asked impatiently. "I've been waiting fo' evaaah!"

"Sorry," she apologized. "I lost track of time."

"Ah, never mind," she dismissed, turning to the door as Tony strolled in. "About time," she called out, receiving a lusty smile in return as he made his way to the men's locker room.

Dana waited for him to leave before taking her hair down, fluffing it, and pulling out a pocket mirror to dab at her makeup. It made May uncomfortable how open they were about sex. At the workplace of all places, too; didn't these weirdos have homes?

"Someone may be watching," May dared complain. "There are cameras everywhere."

"Not in the locker rooms," Dana replied with a smirk. "That's where all the fun stuff happens; feel free to come see for yourself if you want to fuck someone other than a weird hobo." With that, she quickly followed Tony down the hallway and disappeared.

May shook her head in disbelief before settling behind the counter. She picked up one of Dana's fashion magazines and flipped through it while trying to focus on the colorful dresses and elegant models. Despite her best efforts to distract herself, her mind continued drifting back to Dana and Tony.

At least the rain had returned and violently lashed at the front doors, more than drowning out any noises. Still, after fifteen minutes of blankly staring at the same page, knowing they were boinking not two dozen steps away, her curiosity won. After all, she'd been invited! Also she maybe, possibly, might be doing this sort of thing with Sam soon, a little *analytical* preview might do them both some good. She closed the flimsy paper resolutely, creeping gingerly on her toes toward the locker room even as she screamed at herself for it.

Halfway down, she heard sounds. Faint at first, but louder with each step, and soon loud enough to be distinct, recognizable. She listened to the wet, sloppy sounds repeating in a steady rhythm, punctuated by sharp indrawn breaths. Breaths that only broke in their excited hiccup to sputter into a curse or startled, baritone laugh. May froze in front of the door, the Rubicon, standing painfully still as she stared at the simple barrier. Tony's voice was clear now.

His low, manly voice.

"Oh fuck! No, don't stop now. Oh, yeah . . . yeah that's a good little . . . oh! Choke on it!"

Her heart raced while she slowly wedged the door open and poked her head in. The room was dark except for a single sliver of light, which streamed through the open door, and a single flickering tile bulb. May distinctly saw the coital couple. Naked from the waist down, Tony was leaning on the cold lockers across the far wall, a wide, *victorious* grin on his face. Dana was on her knees while her head bobbed back and forth over his crotch, picking up speed as Tony's breathing steadily sped up. His eyes half closed, his face like a wild animal radiating with untamed lust, moving his hips along with her motions. He reached down his hand, grabbing a fistful of her blonde hair and pushing her face down over his crotch as he was nearing his release. A moment later, he let out a low growling noise and a few moments later Dana pulled away, coughing and drawing in sharp breaths.

May pulled back in shock when Tony's eyes fluttered open and caught sight of the light she had leaked into the room.

"Who's there?" he demanded, his voice angry and commanding. "Oh, well if it isn't May?" he asked, suddenly sounding frighteningly normal with the sharp shift in tone upon seeing her. Too normal for a man with his dick out and a half naked girl on the floor in front of him. "Well don't be shy, come on in and join the party" he said in a voice oozing with honey and lingering danger.

With a racing heart, May slammed the door and fled down the hallway. She returned to her post, picked up the magazine, and forced herself to stare at its pages pretending that hadn't just happened. Positively stewing in mortification, she prayed silently for this night to end.

"Well, aren't you a naughty little girl?" Tony's words made her nearly rip the magazine in her hand in half. She drew a quick breath, desperately trying to think of a rebuttal, but he spoke again. "Peeping, really? What are you? One of those repressed virgins who turned into a complete freak?" he asked with a breathy chuckle, quiet, but loud so close to her ear. He had leaned over the desk, bracing himself with an arm on the other side of her body. It made him just one motion away from cornering her completely against the wall.

May felt a tingling ache pulsate in her nether regions as she could hear the pulse in her ears from both fear and forbidden excitement, unable to keep her words straight.

"Ga-go away," she managed, the arousal she felt suddenly disgusting, shameful. God help her if he stuffed a hand in her pants and felt how wet she was, *that* would make everything so much worse! Would he? Was he going to rape her? Would Dana help if she screamed; would she even recognize it as a cry for help? Oh God.

"Are you sure you want me to go? You don't want me to do . . . something else?" he teased, chuckling that deep brooding chuckle again.

He saw that she was nervous, of course he did. And she should be! She was a virgin, Dana had guessed, and she had an eye for those things. Shit, had he ever fucked a virgin? And such a cute one too . . .

"Yes, p-please go away," she asked, sounding strained, on the verge of tears.

Her innocent fear excited him, and that deep, bottomless urge grew in him again. May saw his eyes darken while looking at her with a hungry penetrating gaze. She tried to pull back as he closed up to her.

A sudden slam of a door in the hallway seemed to pull him back to reality. He straightened and backed up a couple of steps just as Dana came around the corner, smacking her lips while trying to reapply her lipstick. "Hey, what are you two up to?" she asked absently, trying to catch her reflection in the glass of the door. "Nothing," Tony answered. "I was just asking if May wanted to join us in our . . . fun. Unfortunately, it seems like she is taking a rain check this time," he said with a grin on his face and a deep chuckle.

Tony disappeared with Dana beside him in the direction of the locker rooms again. May sat still as stone in her chair; she still didn't feel safe around him. She made a mental note to herself that she would make sure to not be alone with him again; for all she knew, he only backed off because Dana was near.

CHAPTER 6

The cookies were still hot from the oven, delicious, dripping with butter and honey. Soft in the middle and crusty at the edge, with crushed walnuts to help the flavor. May baked the cookies herself, using an old recipe her mother had created. They used to bake them every Sunday morning when May was little, and then eat the still-warm cookies at the kitchen table with a big glass of milk. She still remembered the little handwritten note her mother had made her.

Start by preheatin' your oven to a cozy 350°F. Take a bowl and whisk together a heapin' cup of flour, a smidgen of bakin' powder, and a dash of salt. In another bowl, cream together half a cup of softened butter, the same of honey, and a half cup of brown sugar until it's smooth as silk. Beat in a large egg and a splash of vanilla. Slowly blend in your dry mix, then fold in a generous cup of crushed walnuts. Drop spoonfuls of this delightful concoction onto your bakin' sheet, and bake 'em for about 10-12 minutes, until they're golden like a sunset. While they're still warm from the oven, brush 'em with a mix of melted butter and honey for extra love.

May had loved them for as long as she could remember. Everything felt better munching on the childhood treat, even more so with Sam here. They stood on the balcony with a plate full of cookies on the patio table between them, looking out from the perch where Ed had stood with Mary on the day she first arrived. She had their treat waiting by the time her date arrived. He seemed to enjoy them, licking the honey off his hands with his eyes closed in ecstasy. His smile was certainly cheerful.

"Oh my God," he praised in between bites. "I think I might just be in love with you already."

"Don't tease me, Sam," she said sulkily. "You shouldn't throw words like that around!"

They both settled into an uneasy silence at that. After the other day at the movies, they had met a few more times in the woods, once at the diner, and even up at the crossroads where he used a stop sign to flag down cars for cheap flowers. She had never invited him home until now. With Aunt Randa out of town, and Ed still missing since their most recent fight, they had the whole house to themselves.

"Hey, Sam?" she started, breaking the awkward silence.

"Yeah?" He stared at her, expecting something. She wasn't sure what it was, but she noticed his gaze had grown more intense. His eyes drifted down to her lips before bouncing back to her eyes. His own full lips a bit more pressed than usual.

"Kiss me, Sam," she requested softly, even quieter than her default tone, as if too timid to raise her voice.

"What?" he asked uncertainly in a voice just as quiet. "Are you sure? The last time I . . ."

"Kiss me now," she demanded. "Please, I want to."

"Okay," he agreed, slowly cradling her cheek and leaning in to press his lips firmly to hers. Unsatisfied, she gripped him by the collar and pulled him closer, parting her own lips as her eyes fluttered close. It was overdue, but she was shy and he was hesitant to press after her last reaction. The experience was delightful for both of them though. His kiss carried the flavor of the succulent cookies they had shared, and she tasted just as sweet. She wrapped her arms around him, kissing him passionately. His grip on her waist tightened as he pulled her closer, greedily sucking at her lips while she trembled in his embrace.

When they broke apart, they were both winded with excitement. She felt bolder and more adventurous. She kissed him on the hand, giggled, and closed in to kiss his neck while nuzzling up to him.

"What—" There was no time for another word. May cut him off as she pounced on him again. She wanted more; she wanted *everything*, to make love to him all night. The picture of Tony and Dana half naked in the locker room appeared in her head. She felt the lust growing in her.

"No one is here," she whispered enticingly in his ear. "Stay the night with me; we can have the house to ourselves."

"I . . . *fuck*, I can't." He opened his eyes slowly, uncertain of her response.

"Why?" she asked, unable to keep the disappointment out of her voice.

He looked up at the darkening sky.

"I have to go home now; I'm sorry, I-I shouldn't have even stayed out *this* late," he said, breath quickening as he suddenly pulled away from her.

"But today's a Saturday," she protested. She was close to tears and unsure of his sudden change in behavior. "What's so urgent?" she asked, knowing damn well it wasn't like he had a boss who would chew him out for not selling enough flowers.

"I . . . can't," he insisted stubbornly, words growing hard even as his body grew stiff as a statue. The way he bounded to his feet was alarming, too; she could see him growing frantic, the motions seemed unnatural. "I'm sorry . . . I . . . I have . . . to go." Without waiting for her, he bolted downstairs and out the door.

"Sam, wait!" she called, following after him.

Something was wrong, *seriously* wrong. Was it an allergic reaction? Some sort of mental illness? Whatever the case, it didn't seem safe to leave him alone. Already he was beyond the yard; before she could even exit the porch, he was fleeing down the dirt track back toward the woods. She followed him, wondering at his sudden erratic behavior while he raced away.

At the crossroads behind the old town hall, she watched him stumble and land on his knee. Though what stuck out was seeing him bounce back up without even breaking stride, like he was lighter than air. He did it again, even as his next fall left his right foot looking mangled, but even *that* didn't slow him down as he sprinted into the darkening woods.

She followed him and stopped at the edge of the forest, contemplating whether she should follow. Curiosity, but mostly concern, trumped her fear and caution. May ran into the woods. Suddenly, she found herself in a new world of darkness and ominous shadows, the massive trees towering over her like titans. Every branch seemed a grasping hand and every tangled root a nest of snakes or a pile of buried bones.

Nobody ever talked about how just plain *dark* the countryside could get at night.

It was eerie.

She hurried along using her phone as a flashlight. She held it high above her head to provide a little light, but the woods as a whole were invisible in a darkness that seemed to devour the meager light from her cellphone. A darkness with substance to it, like a wall; it almost felt like she could touch it.

It was hard to say if the noise helped or hurt. The forest was alive with sound as its nocturnal denizens composed their night-time symphonies. The chirping of crickets, the distant call of a mating raccoon, and the sound of leathery wings as bats fluttered through the tree branches above her in search of fruit or bugs or blood.

And just ahead of her, shrouded in the deep gloom of the woods, was Sam; she could just barely see him through the darkness, but she could hear the ragged sighs of his labored breathing all too well. The soft rustle of leaves and broken branches as he struggled through the woods, limping heavily, and gasping as if in great pain.

"Sam!" she called after him. "Sam. Please wait, I think you need medical attention!"

He called out through the gloom.

His voice was wrong, and not just because it was so much louder than normal.

"Go back, May." It sounded like a raspy croak, oddly inhuman. He continued running in silence, hoping to lose her in the woods but blazing such a trail even she could see it.

She slowed down to catch her breath while following the trail.

Hearing another gasp and a sharp crash of a fall, she raced forward again, even as her lungs screamed at her to stop. Sam was lying face up in a hollow beside a large oak with partially exposed roots. His head, arms, and legs were visible, but the rest of his body was hidden beneath a heap of dry brown leaves and other vegetation. As she drew closer, his features were obscured even more by the foliage than by the darkness. He groaned softly as she bent down and touched him. Looking over him in such dim conditions was incredibly difficult, but she had to try. Or should she just call 911?

It was then the wings burst out.

They seemed almost like leaves, May discovered as she involuntarily touched them. Backing up, she could see that they were three feet long and two feet wide, brown, furry almost, with bright orange dots scattered across them.

His beanie slipped off and when he raised his head to her, May froze in shock as blood drained from her face.

"May?" he slowly groaned, flipping his eyes open.

Only then did she recover herself. That of all things, seeing that inhuman face speak so *normally,* was what got her body moving. Screaming with horror, she scrambled away on all fours, not stopping until she was a safe distance from him. Without a thought, she turned to stare one more time. To look one more time at the man-sized bipedal humanoid moth with it's brown head, gray wings, and eyes the color of molten gold.

Those eyes that stared right at her as she fled.

CHAPTER 7

In her dreams, he always took the appearance of a moth now. Gold and brown and large as life, or sometimes small and fragile, like a real bug. Whichever size he came in, he always flew away just before she woke up, fluttering higher and higher into the sky until he was lost in the bright glare of the sun. Almost every night since that cookie date, she had the same dreams, and even her waking hours were not spared those memories.

She could never forget the blind chase through the woods, the inhuman sounds he had made as he stumbled on. The way his voice *distorted*. Most of all, she remembered the thing she had held in her arms, buried under a heap of dead brown leaves. The strange furry form that she had touched. It was almost two weeks now, and the nightmares still endured, melding into her waking consciousness.

She threw open the curtains to let some daylight in, washing every dark alcove of her room in its brightness. It reminded her she was awake and drove off the last vestiges of nightmare. She took a shower, ate the light breakfast Maggie prepared without request, and dressed for work in silence; all while listening to Ed *loudly* make love to Mary. Mary seemed to practically live here whenever Aunt Randa was out of town.

Frank never brought his sexual conquests home; he'd rather spend the night at the office with two or more girls of questionable virtue who catered to his every need. So he described it anyway. At least this morning he was home and sober enough to drop her off again; Ed always looked so angry to be asked. Usually he just told her to take his car herself, or walk.

May sat in silence staring forlornly at the sky as the blue truck bumped its way along the road. Her dark and gloomy thoughts gathered like storm clouds. The wind whistled sharply and blew in the open car window, sending cold shivers up her spine. She dissociated, too lost in thought and emotions.

Her Sam hadn't turned up at the clinic in weeks, nor had she caught him anywhere in town. Not even on the roadside where he made his living, and she'd checked there three times now. He didn't answer or return her calls. *Why would he?* she asked herself so often. She had frozen at the sight of the giant humanoid moth lying on the ground. The eyes were the most startling thing about that form, for in those gilded orbs, she sensed total recognition. It was still her Sam, there was no doubt.

His voice had sounded like he was in utter agony, and she ran!

Guilt stewed inside her as she remembered the intense despair she saw in his eyes, the flicker of heartache as she turned and fled from him. She was still lost in these thoughts when the truck pulled into the driveway at the MCMC. Her body was on autopilot walking into the building and settling in at her desk without a word to anyone. Dana was out, and wouldn't be back until the afternoon shift. She had the whole desk to herself. That, at least, gave her a sense of relief. Ever since that fateful night with Tony in the locker room, there was an awkward air between them.

She felt forlorn. Like there was a hole in her heart, a great longing and a cavernous emptiness that Sam had occupied. The white marble tiles on the floor and walls seemed dimmer. The air felt colder, the whole world seemed daunting and unfriendly. Another Tuesday afternoon went by and like each one over the past month, she was miserable. She sorely missed him walking to her desk, just before the start of her lunch break, with a white tulip in his hand and a warm smile spread across his boyish features.

May smiled fondly at the memory. Even the thought of that sparked a little warmth in her heart. She had come to anticipate it, subconsciously watching for him, her eyes naturally flashing to the front door for any sign of his presence. Just like the weeks before, he never appeared. She'd even checked with the records, on the off chance she'd ever missed him.

Why did she feel this way? She had always told herself that dating was for fun, that she was only here for a few years at most, anyway, until she got her nest egg saved. She just wanted to have a man in her life, *any* man! So why was she so hung up on Sam? She didn't expect to miss him like this, miss his deep baritone voice, tenor laugh, the warm, stuffy smell of his sweater. She loved how his hair smelled like summer leaves, wet earth, and wood smoke. It startled and horrified her to realize that she had all these details etched deep in her mind.

Now she knew what he was, but it was there at work, alone with her thoughts, that she decided it didn't matter anymore. She missed him with a passion she didn't know herself capable of.

May realized she couldn't wait another week not knowing if she'd ever see him again.

CHAPTER 8

After work, May journeyed into the woods for the first time since that horrifying night. It was a cold and dreary evening with a light drizzle, just heavy enough to soak through her sweater and dampen her already bad mood. Miserable. After losing her way twice, retracing her steps, and more than a few curses, she located the spot Sam fell.

He wasn't there. She cupped her mouth and called out for him as loud as she could and then waited.

Damp and cold, she stood there defeated, admitting she didn't have the faintest idea how to search for him in these woods. If she wandered off at random she might get lost and literally freeze to death, and that wouldn't help anyone. She turned to leave for home.

The next day she made a fresh start on her search, this time with the sun high in the sky. She managed to travel further into the woods, deeper than ever before. She searched without success until the sun began to set. She resolved to come back tomorrow to try again. It helped that she felt him, somehow. She could feel he was close, just choosing to be elusive. Or maybe that was her head playing tricks on her.

Her mind was certainly frazzled, and more than a little irritated, too, come her next shift. All she could think about was getting back to the woods and continuing the search for her absent boyfriend. It was actually his absence that Dana commented on.

"I haven't seen your serial killer around for a while now. Is he finally in jail?" she teased.

"He's out of town for some business," May lied without thinking.

"What business is that I wonder?" Dana asked in contemplation. "Probably hiding cause the cops are combing the woods for him again," she mocked lightly.

"Whatever he does is his business!" May barked, her frustration turning to anger. "Why don't you mind yours? And don't you ever call him a rapist or a serial killer ever again! It's fucked up!"

"What? Are you serious right now?" Dana asked, seeming to grow defensive by the sudden aggressiveness in her voice. "You're scolding me? For that . . . creep? You two deserve one another," she snapped before turning to go, leaving May with her brooding thoughts.

She didn't mean to have an outburst, but Dana had gotten on her last nerve, and she couldn't help but react. Of late, she had found the older girl's comments too rude and insensitive to bear. This had been the last straw; the wound she had in her heart for Sam was still too raw to go poking at.

Finally left alone with her mind free to wander off wherever it pleased, she returned to that afternoon she had spent with him picking flowers in the sunlit grove. And the day they had ridden the bus to Springfield to see a movie and came back soaked and shivering. She smiled dreamily as the memories came flooding back.

Above her head, a pair of gray moths fluttered around the empty room, seeming to play around the light bulbs in the ceiling.

"You guys haven't happened to come across Sam, have you? Good looking guy, gray wings, big golden eyes, and the most ridiculous sweaters you'll ever see?" She felt stupid talking to the insects, but a very real part of her worried they would respond. After her encounter in the woods, she couldn't truly discount anything, no matter how unlikely.

If they understood her, they didn't have an answer, or just didn't care enough to reply. Instead, they continued to fly at the luminaires with unwavering intensity. She swiped lazily at them to send them off, but they returned, fluttering insistently to the lamp. An incredibly strange idea blossomed in her mind.

CHAPTER 9

The last light of the day had long vanished when she got back to the edge of the forest. The air was cold, windy, and still smelled of rain. The moon illuminated only the faintest, pale silver sheen, barely piercing the thick canopy of leaves to the forest floor.

May steeled herself for the trek. She hadn't noticed the sinister mien of the trees that lined the edge of the woods like an army of gnarled wooden giants. A part of her really hated this forest.

The very air seemed to frown menacingly over her as an unwelcome guest. She sucked in a breath, taking hurried strides into the dark woods, even knowing the idea was a long shot, downright foolish, really. The comfort of her room back home called out to her, but no, she had to see this through. The brick-sized lamp above her head glowed brilliant as a lighthouse beacon in the forest, a high luminosity tool that she'd gone out of her way to buy, providing all the light she needed to navigate over the gnarled roots and fallen trunks.

A light rain drizzled, but the thick canopy of evergreen trees worked like nature's umbrella. Besides, in theory, the device was waterproof; it was designed for camping. The drops dripped down broad leaves and ran down the tree's bark, hitting her and the lamp, but neither failed. It had grown significantly chillier since she started her night-time trek; she could even see her breath in the cold air.

In the forest area known locally as Wood's End, there were no wolves, big cats, or gators—only black bears, which were nearly tame in the region. Even knowing this, May still found herself flinching at the faintest rustling sounds, sure some black bear was just out of sight, melding with the shadows. Hell, running into an actual monster seemed at least possible. It was a stressful, long trek through the dark woods to find the stream she recognized from their first date, walking along the makeshift marker until she found the little grove behind a huge blackberry bush.

She found a natural shelter between the blackberry bush and the rocky outcropping she remembered, a big stone beside the stream that blocked most of the rain. There, quickly, she began gathering the dryest leaves and sticks she could find, trying desperately to build a fire. The cold was hitting her harder than expected, making her weak and her head foggy. She needed warmth.

A while later, she huddled beside the faint orange flame, covering herself in the blanket she had brought. Warily, her eyes scanned the underbrush around her for any sign of Sam, or any other uninvited creatures. One never knew what a bright light might attract at night in the middle of the woods. It was a risky gamble she was making. May was betting on Sam's moth instincts to attract him to the bright light of her lamp, hopefully before anything else found her.

She could see a host of small bright eyes in the murky undergrowth staring back at her. The light reflected small disk-sized orbs; owls, badgers, or other small, nocturnal rodents. She hoped so anyway. Part of her couldn't help but wonder how long it would take the larger creatures to come out and play, if there really were man-eating monsters out here. May closed her eyes, huddling closer to the fire while shivering from both cold and fear.

Her wait was harrowing. The cold was un-pleasant, even huddled next to her small fire. She listened to the rhythmic *rap-tap* of dripping rain on the rock beside her and the low rumble of the stream, the noise strangely calming. Too calming even, as it became increasingly difficult to keep her eyes open. Until finally, unable to fight the sleep any longer, she folded herself under the blanket and closed her eyes. The deep roar of the swollen stream rumbled in her head as she drifted off.

* * *

She woke surrounded by darkness.

It was cold. Her lamp had run out of batteries or something; it was dimmed heavily, and the fire was just smoldering embers. It took her a moment in the waning light to notice that someone stood over her. She shot upright to her elbows, panicked, until she realized it was Sam. Even then, every nerve tingled. He wasn't the gold-eyed winged creature; it was her Sam, the bright-eyed, bright-smiled young man with the silly red beanie.

He wasn't smiling now.

His stare was intense. She couldn't tell what she saw in those penetrating brown eyes. There was sadness, hurt, and mistrust. There was also a deep longing combined with desire. Despite this, she found her attention shifting to the cute laugh lines at the corner of his eyes. She remembered the way they always crinkled up whenever he teased or made fun of her. It was the prettiest sight she had seen in weeks.

She wanted to see him smile, laugh! She wanted to cry, hug, and press her face against his shirt that always smelled of sweat, moss, and mildew. To do *anything* to break this painful silence. It was all she could do not to get up and run into his arms, her heartache increasing ten-fold at the sight of him.

Suddenly, her eyes welled up and hot tears began to stream unbidden down her face, blurring her sight. She sobbed violently while her body shuddered. She couldn't recall the last time she had cried so hard. Did she have full body sobs like this ever, even at her mother's funeral? No, but she *wept* now, out of relief and deep longing, hitting her like an avalanche of pent up emotions bottled up in her heart.

He watched her weep, quiver, and quake but made no immediate attempt to comfort her. Her heart began to sink as he ignored her discomfort. May was just beginning to fear the worst when he knelt to wrap a hand protectively around her shoulder. She took a deep breath of his scent, and finally relaxed in the smell of him, the smell she loved so much. A smile even grew as he used a sleeve to wipe her tears, calming her cries. He smiled back, but didn't rush her to stop her staggered breaths. They sat together for a long time without a word as he held her in his arms, gently stroking her hair while she fought to calm down.

"I should have told you," he offered, after she finally caught her breath. "I wanted to tell you but . . . I was scared. I was just too much of a coward. I didn't want to lose you," he admitted forlornly. As he spoke, his voice was oddly flat.

"I don't want to lose you, either," she conceded, her head nestled snugly against his chest. "I shouldn't have run away like that, I-I don't know why I did!"

"It's to be expected. I've seen my reflection before; I know it's fucking freaky looking," he half-joked.

"That's not true," she insisted, hitting him playfully on the chest. "You're beautiful, Sam. Both forms."

"Thank you, May," he said, not sounding particularly convinced and both fell into another silence.

"So . . . what are you?" she asks after a while. "Are you really human?"

"In many ways, I am. Most ways, I'd argue," he replied, running his hands along her neck, then her back. "I have a heart, like most humans. Can't you hear it?"

"I can," she assured, nuzzling her head into his chest. She listened to the slow steady beat of his heart, which somehow matched the rhythm of hers. "Then how did you . . .?" she trailed off uncertainty.

". . . become this *monster*?" he finished her sentence with a smile. He took her hand in his and intertwined his fingers. "What does it mean to be truly human, I've wondered. I can never get a satisfying answer. I was born a normal boy, then I hit puberty, and started to change and feel different. All sounds pretty normal from there, right?" he asked, his smile growing sad. "Of course, while *normal* boys grew beards and mustaches, I grew furry wings and the antennae. Still, I feel like I'm mostly human, six days a week at least. It's just on Sundays, after the sun goes down, that I transform into a moth. I'm drawn to a strange green light in the woods that puts me into some kind of trance; sometimes I see things, visions, usually I just conk out for most of the night." He paused to take a deep breath, giving May a chance to interrupt if she had any questions. "My family comes from an unbroken line of people like me that runs back centuries I'm told. Honestly, I don't know a whole lot about the history, though." There was a great sadness in his voice; it broke her heart and for a while, she sat speechless, listening to the slow beat of his heart and the faint whisper of his breath.

"How do you not know the history?" she eventually asked, curiosity winning out.

"My great, great, great . . . Maybe four greats, whatever, some old ancestor of mine kind of . . . forced his way into the bloodline. The long lineage is connected to some Native American tribe that, as far as I can find, doesn't exist anymore. Gramps was just some white asshole who raped a woman from the tribe and demanded his son when he discovered that he existed. Shit got really scary around adolescence for *that* particular ancestor, but he still managed to live long enough to have some kids. Half a dozen generations, a few witch burnings, a *lot* of moving, and my immediate family is now the only moth folk I know of."

"I'm so sorry, Sam," she offered, unsure what to say. "I'm sorry you had to carry a secret like this."

"Yeah, I'm sorry, too," he muttered. "For starting a relationship with you, being like this,"

"Don't say that, Sam!" she said with quiet venom. "You're perfect the way you are, you hear me? There's more human in you than half the men I've met."

"Thank you for saying that," he offered, gratitude plain in his voice. "You have a good heart, May. A pure and gentle soul, innocent and unblemished." His voice grew almost hazy, reverent at the words.

"You know, Sam," she began softly, after a long pause. "I think I might be in love with you," she admitted, feeling him grow tense at the words. She could hear his heart begin to beat faster, matching her own.

"I think I love you, too, May," he replied. "I've never been able to be this close to someone, I've never had someone outside my family care about me like you've shown."

She pulled away to look into his face. There was a soft passion in his eyes like she had never seen before. There was also uncertainty, like he feared she would flee again, or that somehow he would lose her. It felt right to kiss him.

Without restraint, she pushed herself into him, her mouth melting into his. She pushed deeper, shuddering as their tongues collided with his startled response. She worked her tongue around his, marveling at the sheer sweetness in his mouth while tugging at his clothes, running her hands through his thick brown curls, and scratching at his back with a fiery hunger building up in her loins.

Unable to contain it, unable to endure how slow he was moving, she straddled him. He ripped open her shirt, popping buttons and revealing a pair of c-cup sized breasts. Her nipples felt so hard. She shivered as the cold breeze blew briefly against her chest, longing for contact. Sam just stared at her bare boobs with a deep hunger gleaming in his eyes, appreciating the sight with his intense gaze, but only for a moment. Then he cupped them in his hands, squeezed gently, feeling the sensitive nipples hard against his palms with quiet reverence.

He leaned in to work on them harder, flicking his tongue across a nipple while rubbing the other between his thumb and forefinger. She stiffened tight as a bowstring. Her breath trembled like fiery tendrils were running up her spine at the sheer intensity of the sensation. He was playing her like an instrument and she had never experienced anything like it.

Just when she thought she couldn't take it anymore, Sam flipped her over with strong arms and laid her on the blanket. Slowly, he stripped off the last of her clothes. She felt vulnerable and excited in equal measure, lying here in the unfamiliar woods, bare naked, but with Sam's body to keep her warm. Despite the locale, she knew she was safe and secure in his arms; it felt she was right where she belonged. There was nowhere else she'd rather be, at least. Sam had awakened a fiery passion in her that had to be sated. It was with that thought she forced his face to hers and kissed him afresh.

He enthusiastically responded. Though he slowly worked his way down after a few minutes, pecking along her neck, then her breasts then her belly before finally settling between her legs. May shuddered, chest heaving heavily as goose prickles crept up her skin. She could feel his hot breath closing in.

Then, his kissing landed between her legs and the whole world disappeared. There were no more trees dripping water, no more fire or lamp or hard ground under her, only the intense sensations emanating from Sam's mouth and the womanhood it was covering. Even the static of the rushing river disappeared. There was only his mouth, wet and warm, his tongue reaching and probing and exploring and devouring every hidden corner of her pussy.

May arched her back, writhing in the throes of a pleasure she had never felt before. She closed her eyes, focusing on the way the sensation grew, intensified in her loins seemingly without limit. The fire built inside her. Dexterous fingers crawled up her body delightfully as tears streamed down her face. She started to buck, pull away as if stopping this wasn't the *last* thing she wanted, but his grip was strong and kept her securely pinned under him.

It was amidst this spasming she reached the peak; she could not stop it. Her whole body shuddered from the release, tensing in mind-melting pleasure as if something was snapping inside her. Her eyes closed as her ragged breath changed into short quivers. Her legs felt like noodles, too weak to stand on, let alone walk.

Fortunately, she wanted nothing less than to leave.

CHAPTER 10

The sky brightened into a deep cobalt as the first light of day crept up the eastern horizon and penetrated the foliage.

Under the trees, May stirred from the sweetest sleep she had been blessed with in a long time, even waking to the sight of her breath misting in the cold morning air. The frigid cold mornings of early winter were becoming more common as autumn ended. She sat up beneath her half-frozen blanket, looking around at a forest turned to crystal.

The pale pink light of dawn sparkled off branches, leaves, and stones in a breathtaking display. The green grass stood stiff like flat chips of emerald from the frozen dew, which glittered like a thousand tiny diamonds. Flowers and mushrooms alike were covered with thin layers of ice. Even the ugly mud puddles left by the rain had a slight sheen to their surface.

The daytime denizens of the woods began to wake. Birds twittering in the treetops, while squirrels scurried across branches to fight over who would get the first nuts.

Sam was gone.

He had disappeared during the night. She had fallen asleep wrapped in his arms with her face pressed snugly against his chest and was *very much* missing the warmth of his strong body. Sitting alone, in the bitter cold while her nocturnal companion was nowhere in sight made her uneasy.

She looked around briefly for any sign of him with no luck. The only proof she had that it had not all been a dream were the ashes of their fire and their shared sleeping area. She looked around in uncertainty, now wondering if she had somehow hallucinated the whole evening. Was she feverish, sick from the cold, not in her right mind?

Then she saw it, lying on the blanket beside her, a crimson-colored beanie with a red pompon at the top. May sighed in relief. Pressing the simple cloth to her chest helped her remember his smile, one that was both dreamy and naughty. It reminded her that it was real.

* * *

It was a bright morning that saw her arrive at the office. The air was cool from the previous night's rain, but the sun felt warm on her skin. Maybe it was just the placebo effect of that golden orb shining down from a cloudless, blue sky, making winter seem that much weaker. Maybe it was just her good mood. May felt lighter than air, like she could fly if she tried!

Inside the nursing room, she stripped off her clothes to change into her uniform. It was still about fifteen minutes before work began, giving time for her to check herself in the mirror before his visit. She had never paid much attention to her body, more concerned with her face and its weird pug nose. It always seemed like the first thing people noticed about a woman was her face.

After last night's fun, she found herself checking out her body, studying the curves, crevices, and cuts in her young form. She had always been a skinny child—skinny arms, scrawny neck, skinny legs, and no waist to speak of. As she grew older, her hips widened while her thighs thickened. The little buds on her chest grew until she could no longer cup them completely in her hands. Without thought, she found herself cradling them in her palms and pushing them upright, blushing slightly as she remembered Sam's tongue on them.

It was with that soft blush she turned around to check her side profile, slightly arching her back to emphasize the curve of her butt. Slowly, she ran her hands down her slender neck, along her prominent collarbones, and across her breasts, tracing the path of his kisses. She drew her fingers over the protruding points of her nipples jutting out from beneath her light silken chemise. She was flushed red by the time she was done reminiscing. Experi-mentally, May clamped her fingers firmly on her hard nipple and gasped at just how good it felt. She ran the other hand down her belly, over her mound, and between her legs. She was shocked at the wetness she felt as her fingers slid inside herself, building her pleasure. Slowly, delicately, she moved her digits in and out and through her lips.

It helped to close her eyes, trying to recreate the sensation of his lips, the sights that accompanied her bliss last night. Suddenly, the door crashed open and snapped her out of her reverie. She composed herself, ran fingers through her hair, and steadied her breath just in time.

As if Dana would judge.

She came into view, heading straight for her locker without so much as a word or glance. The awkwardness between them had been growing for some time; after their brief altercation a few days ago, whatever warmth lingered between them seemed completely extinguished. May didn't regret her words exactly, but she still wished for the confidence to break this silence. To say something lighthearted and show that there were no real hard feelings.

She watched the buxom blonde change, covertly observing her in the mirror as she stripped off her clothes. She had seen Dana dressed down before, but this was the first time she had noticed her features in full, bright lighting. She was taller than May, at least six feet of long, elegant limbs. Her breasts were fuller, too, bulging slightly above her brassiere, contrasting sharply with her slender waist, just the same as her wide hips. There was something about her black lace-fringed underwear against the pale white skin that added both a somber and exciting look to her figure. She wondered idly how a girl could fail to achieve her dream of being a supermodel with a body like that.

It just went to show how much of it was dumb luck.

The silence was killing her. Should she just apologize like she was completely in the wrong? Tell her she had a great body, or make another lewd joke about naked nurses in the hold? After a long, silent debate with herself, May chose to keep her mouth shut. They were civil, and that brought with it the fear of making things worse. She dressed quickly and exited the room.

She had barely settled into her desk when a short man walked in dressed like a cowboy. He swaggered to the counter, wide-brimmed hat and all, one that added almost a half-foot to his height. The boots probably contributed to that, too; they were loud on the marble floor, almost like heels. His stunted legs, waddled gait, and childlike size of clothes made him a rather comical sight. He paused at the counter and doffed his hat at her in a mock bow, smiling like some cliché farm boy.

"Hello, nurse," he said in a poorly mimicked frontier accent.

"Hello sir," May said, struggling to suppress her brewing laughter. He looked endlessly comical to her, while emanating a strong air of raunchiness. "How can we help you today?"

"I umm . . . seem to have lost my horse," he said, spreading his arms so she would notice his outfit. "And I am in dire need of a new ride." He placed his hands on her desk and drew himself up toward her, imploring her with heavy-browed eyes. "Would you let me mount you? Just for a little while, I promise not to ride too far," he offered.

"Oh, Thomas," Dana replied, strolling in and speaking with mock sympathy. "I would let you ride *me*, but I'm afraid you're more likely to fall off and break your neck. That would be quite unfortunate, seeing as the pediatrician is off for the day." She smiled sweetly at him and turned back to her desk, returning to her work arranging patient files and the day's appointments.

"Har har," he sneered at her. "I've ridden bigger and hotter horses back in the day. What's a little filly to me?"

"Oh, I'm sure you've ridden them all," May jumped in with a dry smile. "When they aren't looking, or they're fast asleep. I mean, a sneaky little bastard like you, they probably don't even feel it when you slide in," she said, almost surprising herself at the words leaving her mouth. But the annoyance that had suddenly bubbled up in her needed an outlet. And he was begging for it.

"I bet you would," the little man barked, puffing up his chest. "Twenty dollars says you would." He slid his hand into his coat and pulled out a crumpled twenty dollar note and wagged it in her face like it was actually enticing.

"Okay that's enough, I doubt May appreciates being called a whore; get the fuck out or I'm calling the sheriff," Dana interjected. "Fine, bitch, fine I'm going!" he declared, turning to leave. May turned to check on her coworker after the remark, but her eyes crinkled in excitement. The leggy woman had a proud smile on her face as the little man stormed out.

"That was nicely done," she complimented. "I told you you'd learn."

"Thanks," May offered, grateful for the compliment but unsure how to react to the sudden warmth.

"Can I sit here?" Dana asked, indicating the seat.

"It's your seat," May replied to the joke with an awkward laugh, looking at the other girl. "You work here, right?"

"It was only a polite gesture," Dana replied, rolling her eyes. She settled down beside May, the silence returning for a while. Both girls were oddly aware of each other but not sure how to break the spell of their silence. Dana tried first.

"Umm . . . listen, May. I just wanted to . . . uh . . ." she began, a bit unsure of how to proceed. She sounded uncomfortable with what she had to say. "I shouldn't have . . . I mean, that day, I shouldn't have badmouthed Sam like that. That was wrong," Dana admitted, sounding strangely vulnerable, almost childlike. For the first time since May had known her, she seemed her actual age. She seemed so experienced and confident that sometimes it was easy to forget Dana was only in her early twenties, like herself.

"You insulted him plenty of days," May corrected softly, not wanting to re-ignite the fight, but intent on hitting home with her message. "You shouldn't have called him that at all . . . But I shouldn't have snapped at you the way I did . . . I'm sorry. Truce?" she asked hopefully.

"Truce," Dana conceded, shaking May's hand. "We need to celebrate!"

"Uh, okay I guess. Any ideas?"

"Let's go out," Dana suggested. "You know that bar near town hall, Wilbur's? They have a great dance floor; we should go have some fun, just us. No boys, no boy talk, just two hot ladies out on the town; what do you think?"

May didn't expect that. In truth, she wanted to decline. Maybe if Sam joined them it would be fun, but dancing alone or with her friend just sounded daunting. Still, she couldn't afford to refuse the peace offering; the fragile friendship was just mended, and she wanted to strengthen that fix. She had sorely missed this blonde girl with the upbeat vibe helping her pass time at work.

"Yeah, sounds fun!" she finally agreed. "Let's go have some fun, enjoy our Friday." May breathed in Dana's lavender oil as she leaned in excitedly. May reflected on the past week as she fell into her work, grateful for Dana's apology. Not only had she gotten back with Sam, but she'd had her first sexual act, they had spent a magical night together. Now she was making up with her best and only friend here in town.

All seemed right and good in the world for once.

CHAPTER 11

May returned home, and actually found herself somewhat excited about going out with Dana. Ed was in the living room, hauling a large pink suitcase out of the house to his Rover parked in front. There was already a small stack of luggage by the front door where she stood.

Watching him work for a while, intense concentration was clearly engraved on his clean-shaven face. He lifted each box to his chest and tossed it into the open trunk, loading the vehicle while completely ignoring her presence.

"Hello Ed," she offered, hoping to break the tense air.

"Hello May," he growled not even glancing at her, let alone stopping his work.

"So . . . Mary is moving out?" she dared ask. It was difficult to talk to him; she was never sure of his temperament. Usually, he was angry to answer her questions, and today was no exception.

"I'm packing her stuff, aren't I?" he snapped, finally turning to face her. "That ought to make you all happy." She finally got his attention, and now he focused it on her intently. Anger burned behind his dark gray eyes as they bored into hers, as if offered some great insult. As if *daring* her to say another word.

Still, he was being unfair. Aunt Randa didn't want Mary around the house, and hell maybe even Frank, too, but not her! May was beginning to like the freckled, bunny-toothed blonde. Mary was odd, and utterly shameless about sex, but May had come to realize that there was a good heart beneath all that. When sober, she seemed level-headed and reasonable, which granted, wasn't very often. She was maybe the only person May knew capable of keeping up with Frank.

Said bunny woman came down the stairs, wearing a gray top that hung loosely over her immense bosom, a blue miniskirt, and long riding boots. A look of mild reproach settled on her freckled face, even as she smiled at May.

"That's not fair, Ed," she gently chastised. "May has always been nice to me. We all know why I'm leaving, and it's not because of her."

"You're not the one who should be leaving," he grumbled darkly, dragging off another box to the car.

"I'm sorry about him," Mary apologized. "Really, don't let him talk to you that way!"

"He's angry, I get it," May offered. "Why is he always mad? Is it your whole . . . situation?"

"Ed's got a lot to be mad about," the other girl explained with a sidelong look at him. He placed another of her bags gingerly into the truck. She looked like she wanted to explain, opening her mouth without speaking before finally settling on a few more words. "It's hard for him to feel anything else."

"Right," she muttered, unsure what else to say. "So, are you still coming around for the barbeque tomorrow?"

"Your aunt will be there," Mary mentioned with a tired smile. "Not to mention her numerous political and business associates, and the *reverend*." She laughed without humor. "I'm a bar singer, May. God forbid they caught me anywhere near such honorable and dignified guests."

"Yeah 'honorable' men like Frank and the reverend and everyone else who drink themselves sick every night! The *good Christians* who fuck anyone who lets them, usually behind their spouses backs," Ed announced, lifting the last box into the truck. "Fuck them and fuck her. I'm not going either."

"But you have to," May protested. "You're her son. People will look for you and ask questions; they're your family!"

"No. No, they *really* aren't," he began coldly. "Neither are you, for that matter!" he snapped suddenly at her.

"Ed, stop it," Mary demanded, growing angry. "May didn't do anything; you need to apologize." Rather than comply, he grabbed the last suitcase and stalked off. Mary turned back to May, eyes brimming with sympathy. "I'm so sorry."

His words stung as much as his silence and cold treatment, but she could take it. In both their defense, he *was* practically a stranger, just some guy she was barely related to. Shrugging off the insult wasn't all that hard. The looks were the thing that unnerved her. That quiet, ever-present anger in his eyes. Most of all, she hated the look in Mary's eyes, the look of compassion and pity in that gray gaze, like something one felt for a wounded bird or stray dog. She wasn't a stray, she wanted to scold Mary, emphasize that she *really was fine*, maybe even remind her that she could fight her own battles.

Her eyes filled with tears, blurring her vision, and she hated that, too. She hated feeling weak and vulnerable. Unable to look at either of them anymore, she fled up the stairs into her room, shutting the door behind her as Mary called out something she couldn't hear.

She wanted to cry, to crouch in a dark corner and weep until her eyes were sore, or to curl up in her bed and cry herself to sleep. She didn't. Dana was expecting her and she wasn't going to stand up her friend.

May wiped her eyes roughly, blinking back the tears until they dried away. The car engine started and zoomed off while she was changing out of her clothes. It was that signal that let her finally relax, lie in bed, and take a proper deep breath, but she couldn't rest long.

Dana was waiting.

CHAPTER 12

It was long past sundown by the time May arrived at the dancehall.

Another typical Friday for the establishment, at least that was what Dana told her. May hesitated while standing outside the door. The dim lighting, loud music, sparsely clad girls, and the sheer heat of a half-hundred crowded bodies loomed before her threateningly. One of the last places she ever wanted to be; she hated crowds, loud music, and socializing for the most part.

Dana appeared before she had a chance to back out. The dance floor was filled with people boogying to the fast rhythm of the music, some upbeat fiddle song she didn't recognize, as she navigated her way through the crowd of party goers. Dana pulled her to a table, her long platinum hair tied in two tails, contrasting sharply with the deep black, painted on her nails, lips, and around her eyes. Tight latex trousers clung tight to her body, matching her high-soled boots and black leather jacket.

The goth look was unexpected, but Dana wore it well; it suited the chalk-white skin, making her look almost vampiric.

In comparison, May looked like an angel. She wore only a white top under a white jacket with a navy blue skirt that ended just above her calves; the only black she had were leather sandals. Instantly, she felt out of place, out-dressed to a ridiculous degree, especially being bare of any makeup save her usual strawberry lip gloss.

The bemused smile on Dana's heavily painted face did little to assuage her fears.

"Geez, took you long enough to show up!" she mocked, still moving slowly to the rhythm of the beat. "You didn't even get dressed!" she complained further, even as she smiled.

"What's wrong with my clothes?" May asked.

"It's not your clothes that's the problem," Dana began. "Your outfit is okay if you're attending a tea party or some mid-summer picnic. You're in a dancehall, you gotta look the part!" She seized May by the hand and pulled her toward the ladies bathroom.

"Where are you taking me?" May asked uncertainly.

"Don't argue," Dana demanded. "I'm gonna get you fixed in no time!"

Figuring she'd come this far, May followed, wondering what dark magic Dana had planned to make her worthy of this dingy backwater dancehall. In the restroom, there were small stalls on one side and large mirrors on the other. The lighting was a pure white that glared a brilliant reflection in the mirror, making it easy to see what they were doing, at least.

"You stay here," Dana ordered. "I'll be back," she declared, leaving May befuddled. A minute later she returned, carrying a large backpack and a half empty bottle of vodka. Dana took a swig as she studied her new project. "Where do we start . . ."

"Wait, what are you planning?" May asked, even taking a wary step back. "What are you going to do to me?"

"Chill out, May," Dana said dryly. "I'm just going to doll you up a bit." She walked around her as she spoke, giving her clothes a proper inspection.

"Leave it to me. I'll start by building a *big* fire and burning these clothes you're wearing. They deserve to be *punished* for hiding a body like yours." She shook her head ruefully. "But, that'll have to wait. For now, you'll need a proper hairstylist, good makeup, some color on your nails—*look* at those nails," she criticized bluntly, as if the problem was obvious.

May felt squeamish. She turned to observe her reflection in the mirror; her hair was long and slightly tousled, but what of it? She never wore much makeup, but she looked fine! She couldn't for the life of her see what Dana was fussing so much about.

"You need a complete makeover, girl," Dana said. "Luckily, I'm something of a pro!" she bragged, taking a puzzled May into an empty stall and retrieving a smaller bag from within the backpack.

A few shaves, a few cosmetics, and ten minutes later, May walked out of the stall to look at herself in the mirror. She could hardly recognize the woman. Her face had been utterly transformed. Sometime in the last ten minutes, she had lost the haphazard undergrowth around her forehead, her jet-black hair had been combed so fine that it fell long and unbroken across her shoulders. Her lips turned shiny and an alluring shade of crimson.

Dana stepped up behind her.

"Tilt your head a little up," she advised, raising her chin with one hand and pressing the other against the small of her back. "And arch your back a little bit . . . ah! There you go,"

May couldn't help but smile at her reflection. She had never seen herself like this, and while she had always felt queasy when she wore makeup, she had to admit that this was a long way from the nervous girl with the ponytail and hillbilly clothes. She looked good.

"Hey, Dana," she began, still studying her reflection in the mirror. "I wanna . . . umm . . . Can you help me with something?"

"Yeah? What's the matter, lil sis?" Dana asked as she narrowed her eyes in concern. "Tell me what's wrong, you know I got you," she declared, already a little drunk, and taking a small swig from their bathroom vodka despite it.

May didn't want to tell her. It was too embarrassing, unbelievable even, and she didn't really know how much she could trust her blonde colleague. Hell, she didn't even know about the goth getup. Still, she couldn't deny the fact that she wanted to talk this out. A local might have insight that she didn't. May took a deep breath, gathered her thoughts and . . .

* * *

It was almost three hours before they were done, before 'girls' night' ended. The dancehall had gotten rowdier as the partiers got drunker and more erratic. The loud music and dim lighting dulled her senses and the shots of vodka that Dana was pouring down her throat weren't helping.

May had never been so drunk in her life; she barely remembered the night they'd enjoyed. She felt lightheaded, with a sense of weightlessness that almost seemed to float her up off the ground. Her eyes swam, her head felt hollow. The slightest of sounds thundered and echoed inside her head. Not entirely unpleasant but getting worse by the minute.

May decided she didn't like getting drunk.

"It's late, Dana," she said, eyes shut tight to better focus her senses. "I wanna go home."

"Whaaaaat?" the other girl asked, baffled. She had only just got back from the bar with a refill. "The party's just getting started, May!"

"Not for me," she rebutted, staggering in the other direction. "Oh, I think I'm gonna be sick."

"Okay okay, I'll get Frank to drive you home," Dana assured, quickly disappearing, and shocking the inexperienced drunk when she seemed to pull the man from thin air. In reality, he had recently walked in, and Dana simply retrieved him. He looked annoyed, but he led her to his car all the same.

She was fast asleep before they were half a mile from the dancehall.

So much of the night was lost from her mind by the time she slept away her hangover, even her admission to Dana.

CHAPTER 13

The whole morning of her next shift moved at a crawl.

The rain raged outside. It had rained off and on for the last three days, with perpetual dark clouds blotting out the rising and setting sun. May frequently checked her watch and struggled to focus on anything. Time moved faster in her mind than in reality. She was terrified that he wouldn't come, that their night in the woods together wouldn't have changed anything.

At the stroke of one P.M., Sam knocked on the front door and walked in, punctual as ever before but dressed fancier than his usual duds. A black leather jacket over a white turtleneck top, with neatly ironed black trousers and shiny black leather boots made him look like the prince straight out of a fairy tale, even if the red beanie cap on his head looked conspicuously out of place.

He shook the raindrops off his umbrella and wiped his boots on the floor mat before approaching the reception. May kicked her legs in anticipation, safely hidden by the desk. Her eyes flickered to the small bundle of white tulips in his hand until he strolled over and held them out to her.

"Here you go, miss," he said. "One for every week I kept you waiting. White like your person, innocent and unblemished," he said with rehearsed precision.

"You're too sweet, Sam," she replied with a shy smile. "Does innocent still fit though? I seem to crave less innocent things these days."

"And what are these 'less innocent' fascinations of yours?" he asked, leaning on the desk as he picked up her cue.

"Oh, for that you will have to come closer, sir," she teased. "I'm afraid they're not fit for public ears."

He leaned in at that, smiling at her warmly.

"What evils do you have to confess, miss?"

"So many, sir," she said flirtatiously. "I'm ashamed to even say them out loud."

His pink lips were deliciously alluring that afternoon; she found herself staring as she spoke.

"How dreadful," he returned, staring right back. "Are you admitting before me to harboring mischief and mischievous thoughts in your heart?"

"I am, sir," she said, rising slowly and bringing her face closer to his. "I could kiss you now if it weren't for all these cameras."

"You wouldn't find me unwilling, cameras or no," he admitted. "Though I admit all this light makes me a little . . ."

The sudden seriousness in his words gave her pause.

"What?"

Dana cleared her throat loudly as she came to the desk, taking her seat.

"Ah," May said, hiding her annoyance at the interruption. "Sam, you know Dana, my colleague and accomplice. Dana, Sam, whose relation to me is none of your business," she teased, all sharing a brief hearty laugh. Dana smiled sweetly, though there was something in her eye.

"Yes, I know Sam quite well, don't I?" she began. "May has talked a lot about you lately, and I must say, I've been *dying* to chat." She said that last part with a sidelong look at May.

You couldn't help yourself, could you? May thought, mildly amused by the morbid joke. Sam coughed before he spoke.

"It's nice to see you, too, Dana. But I'm afraid we're in the middle of something quite confidential." He turned to May. "Is there somewhere we can speak privately?"

"Yes, come with me." She silently apologized to Dana with her eyes before leading him away with her grip. They headed down the nurse's lobby, slipping into a dark, empty storeroom. "What's the matter?"

He drew a deep, ponderous breath as he worked up the courage to share the news. He chose his words carefully as he began.

"You want me to tell you everything about my . . . condition, right? There's uh . . . something I should really tell you, if so," he mumbled. May felt a sudden tightness in her gut. She didn't like the way this conversation was unfolding. He had never sounded this solemn. What new horror was there in his bloodline that he hadn't yet shared?

"Tell me, what is it?" she asked, the words choking in her throat. He spared a glance over his shoulder at the door, his discomfort palpable.

"You know how I'm a normal person six days a week," he said, looking furtively through the window blinds. "And how on the seventh, I become a . . . uh . . ." he trailed off, seeming to lose his nerve.

"A cute furry moth with beautiful golden eyes?" May finished with a smile. "I already know that, Sam." She did her best to sound soothing, taking his hands in hers to calm him.

"That's not all, May," he insisted trying to smile back.

"Don't tell me you also drink nectar and lay little moth eggs," she teased weakly.

"God, no," he retorted in mock disgust, laughing lightly in surprise.

She continued laughing along with him.

"If you don't drink nectar or lay little moth eggs, what could be so horrible to make you this on edge?" She looked down at their joined hands. "I can't even feel my hands anymore."

He smiled sheepishly but dropped his iron grip in an instant.

"It's not something I can explain easily," he said. "I'd rather show you, but first . . ." He leaned in and kissed her. She could feel her doubts melt away along with all her other fears and insecurities. Suddenly, she felt the softness of his lips, his strong arms around her waist, and not a single thing else.

He broke off long enough to look her in the eyes and smile. "Meet me at the grove tonight, six o'clock."

She only nodded timidly.

* * *

The rain had subsided into a persistent drizzle by the time May reached the edge of the grove.

From there, Sam led her to his home, a surprisingly cozy building of wood logs. Not much larger than a hunter's cottage, but surrounded by all manner of flowers, bushes, and other natural beauty. He had also built a great hanging tent under the trees from twenty square feet of white canvas, protecting his makeshift yard from the elements. A large rocky outcrop protected them from the cold breeze coming from the river, even outside.

Inside was even better. The ground around the fireplace was a patchwork canvas made of fur mats and soft woolen blankets. The ruddy orange glow radiating from the fire made it yet more cozy. Sam stood by the fire, wrapped in a huge woolen blanket and staring blankly into the flames until she entered, turning him around sharply.

"What do you think?" he asked before anything else. She looked up at the supported roof, then at the suspended flaps and open sides of the tent outside. It all looked rudimentary enough to her.

"Of your architecture? Not so much," she announced with a mild chuckle. "Of your hospitality? That I'm yet to see."

"Then come over and let me show you," he goaded, spreading his arms to embrace her in a warm hug as she complied. She let him hold her, melding into him and savoring the warmth of his body pressed against hers. They stood silently for what seemed a long time, entangled in each other's grip with the only sound being the steady dripping of rain on the canvas roof, and the gentle crackle of their fire.

"I've missed you," she whispered into his shirt, realizing how true it was. "I miss you all the time. Every minute of every day."

"I missed you, too, May," he replied, running his fingers through her hair. "And it's hard to explain, but I am completely overwhelmed by you right now."

They were just words, hell, she knew men lied all the time to get what they wanted, but still, she believed him. Was it the calmness of his voice when he spoke, or the slow unhurried beat of his heart that made her believe him so unconditionally? She raised her head to his and her clear, green eyes locked with his.

"Then kiss me like you missed me," she said softly, her breath getting caught in her throat.

They had done it plenty since meeting, but the feel of his lips on hers was still thrilling. There were flavors still left untasted. His mouth was soft and accommodating, sometimes turning strong and insistent without warning. She reveled in the silky smoothness of his tongue. He continued holding her by the waist, slowly running his hands up her back and then down over her behind.

Suddenly, she shuddered.

"Fuck, you're cold," he said with alarm, pulling back from her. "Ah, your clothes are wet!"

"Not wet enough," she teased, trying to brush off his concerns with a lewd remark. "I intend to make them *much* wetter before we're done." She tried to kiss him again, her lust clearly betraying reason.

"Don't be stubborn, May, it's dangerous to be wet out here," he insisted, gently pulling the rain-sodden jacket off her back. "Come sit by the fire; you need to get warm and dry. I won't have you falling sick on me."

She rejoined him in cuddling by the fire, washed in its ruddy warmth with a soft woolen blanket draped over their shoulders. She shivered violently from the cold at first, but the fire worked it's magic quickly on her body, and before long, the color returned to her cheeks. All the while, those soft, strong hands continued stroking her body affectionately. It was then she decided it was time to try out Dana's first lesson.

She shrugged off the blanket, sweeping up to her knees in one fluid motion. Taking care to execute the moves just the way she had practiced, she braced herself across from him, not more than a couple of feet away. He stared at her in wonder as he spoke, sounding amused.

"What are you doing?"

"Nothing" she coyly replied, trying to hide her anxiety. Part of her felt ridiculous crawling around on her knees, but Dana had warned her about that as well. She was the professional seductress after all.

May braced herself and smiled seductively at him from across the fire. She unbound her hair and shook out her long locks, letting them fall heavy across her shoulders before sliding up onto her legs, arching her back slightly and slowly as she untied the laces on her blouse. She gave Sam suggestive glances through the whole little dance.

It was working.

She could see his interest now. His gentle smile was unchanged, but the amusement in his eyes transformed to a deep hunger, an impatience. She carried on with growing confidence. She untied the last ribbon and slowly slipped off the blouse, revealing a pair of perky breasts. She rubbed her fingertips over her pink nipples and through the cleft between them.

His eyes grew from intense to insane, almost manic in their focus on her body.

Did I make him this hot? she wondered, swelling with feminine pride. May felt powerful knowing that she had such a pronounced effect on him. Her eyes felt coy and seductive as she leaned in to speak.

"What are you thinking, Sam?"

He stood up and flashed a savage smile. He yanked her forward and pressed his bulging erection hard against her. It was all she could do not to squeal in anticipation. Her heart was hammering like mad as his husky voice replied.

"You have no idea . . . the dirty things I'm thinking right now."

"Then don't just stand there," she teased. "Be a gentleman and help a lady out of the rest of these clothes."

Sam needed no further convincing. He pounced on her, ripping off the last of her clothes and kissing every exposed inch of her body he could reach. Sam had always seemed calm and deliberate when they made out, but now he ravaged her body with an unprecedented passion, like a beast. He took one of her nipples in his mouth, sucking hard until she whimpered in pain. She gasped as his strong hand slid between her legs and felt the wetness there.

There was a little jerk through her body when his finger slipped through her lips. She gasped and fumbled with his belt to release him as he tore off his own shirt. Seeing her tremble, he reached for the belt and opened it with one hand, pulling it out of the belt loops in one motion, while holding her neck with the other.

He pulled her closer and kissed her neck slowly. It seemed to take ages the way he moved his mouth along her slender neck, while feeling his hot rapid breaths in her ear. She reached down and unzipped his pants before slowly pulling out his penis. She could hardly believe what she was seeing, what she was about to do. It was warm, and harder than she expected, with a deep pulsating throb when her fingers slid around it. At first barely touching him, she just ran her hand slowly along the shaft and up to the swollen head.

He groaned softly as it twitched in her hand.

May wanted it inside her, even if the notion terrified her. She looked up and saw the intense lust in his eyes at the same time as a tenderness and care that seemed to make him hold back his most immediate urges.

"Put it in," she breathed out as her pulse raced.

"Are you sure?" he asked, after kissing her body a good dozen more times, making his words hit thrice as hard.

"Put it in, Sam," she repeated, sucking in her breath. Her hand rubbed eagerly at his cock, squeezing the girthy piece of flesh as she confirmed again, "Make love to me, Sam."

He kissed her forehead before he devoured her neck like a beast again, with a soft grip of her hair. Again, her mind was drowned in pleasure by his affections. Suddenly, he lifted her up with strong arms and laid her on her back on the soft blankets covering the cottage floor. He held her firmly by the waist and adjusted her hips, finally lining himself up between her legs. Her whole body tensed as he rubbed it with the head of his cock. With her mouth slightly open, eyes wide, she waited for the penetration with every nerve in her body tingling.

She was wet, and dripping when he gave it to her. The feel of him going in, sliding smoothly between her nether lips, was like nothing she had ever experienced. A fiercely agonizing sensation ran through her as he thrusted inside. It was excruciatingly uncomfortable in one way, but in another, wickedly pleasurable.

Still, she cried out in pain.

He pulled out, and she shuddered with relief. The second thrust was more manageable, and she only whimpered softly, clamping her eyes tight. The third was smoother still, and the fourth was pure euphoria.

By the fifth thrust, she had adjusted to the rhythm of his strokes and the throbbing hardness inside her. She opened her mouth to speak, but only a weak groan escaped her lips. He was boring deeper into her and reaching places she never even reached with her own fingers. The connection became deeper and deeper still until May almost felt like they became one, moving in unison like a dance. She moved her hips, rocking back and forth to the speed of his strokes until the slaps were like music, unlocking a different pleasure with every note.

She felt the heat rising with the urgency of his strokes. She knew she wouldn't last as long as she did last time. She had learned not to fight the sensation, but rather to embrace it and ride it out like a surfer cresting an ever-growing wave to shore. May knew the wave wouldn't hurt her.

There was a cry of pleasure, quakes, and one more hard jerk with her climax.

His cock twitched inside her. She tensed every muscle in her reach stretching taut. His breath grew faster and more unsteady and suddenly, he exploded. His whole body shuddered from the effect of his release as she felt her inside filling with warmth. They lay silently together as his breath slowed. May put her hands around him as a dull ache lingered in her groin, but it was a sweet ache, a physical reminder of what she'd just experienced.

She relished it in a content bliss.

***

In that very moment, Dana sat shivering beneath a huge oak tree a few yards from the tent.

She entered the forest just before sundown, hard on May's heels, trailing her easily all the way to the grove. Most of May's conversation with her strange boyfriend was lost, just a few whispered words on the edge of hearing, but it was of more consequence to her than any blaring trumpet or war horn. Everything was different now, she could see it, she could hardly believe her luck, but before she got ahead of herself, she needed to be sure. Sure that he really turned into a giant moth.

She needed to see it with her own eyes.

For most of the afternoon, she'd waited at the edge of the woods behind the gnarled trunk of a maple tree. May walking without stealth and carrying a white halogen lamp had made it trivial to evade her sight in the darkness, and easy to track. So, Dana stalked the younger woman through the massive trees, following the bright glow of the lamp but keeping a safe distance between them. The trail took her southward along a gentle sloping ridge to an icy river rushing with a loud rumble. The next route took them downstream along the bank. She shivered violently from the breeze from the water, pulling her cloak tighter as she followed the distant light.

Time and time again, the other girl would stop suddenly, looking furtively around her. As if May sensed somehow that she was being followed, but Dana was well-equipped to hide, melting into the gloom-covered undergrowth with her dark outer wear.

It was after sundown by the time they got to the edge of the secluded grove north of the riverbank. The woods around had grown dark; she could barely see her feet but within the grove, sheltered between a huge blackberry bush and a rocky outcropping, was a small homestead. Lights suspended from overhanging branches were giving her sight of the destination.

It was only now, after they had had fallen silent, that she dared to come closer.

Dana peeked inside and saw their sweaty bodies still entwined in carnal passion, glimmering in the ruddy glow of the fire. She watched Sam crouch naked between his partner's legs. His massive chest heaving heavily as he thrusted deeply inside the lucky woman under him. His hands wrapped firmly around her waist to control the rhythm of their energetic lovemaking.

May lay under him with her back arched as she rocked with his strokes. She was overwhelmed; Dana could see it even from where she hid. Her eyes were clamped shut; her lips parted but silent in their gasping cries until her whimper grew into a breath-quivering moan as his strokes got more insistent and the pace built.

Dana continued to watch from the safety of her shadows. She was hot, her ears burned as the heat rose to her face. She could see Sam's sleek abs and flanks as they tensed and loosened with each swaying motion. The sound of his rugged, manly grunts was staggering. She could feel her sensation grow with theirs, the build-up to their climax as arousing as the sight of their naked bodies.

Climax came for them as May neared her peak. She saw Sam sag as he let out a shuddering moan, May jerking sharply under him, her toes curled outward as he filled her with his cum. Then they collapsed into the makeshift rug, bodies tumbling in a tangle of sweaty limbs.

Dana was frozen behind a bush, just now daring to breathe. The show had flustered and winded her. She reached between her legs and felt the sticky wetness there. It was absurd and queerly exciting that she watched her friend having sex with *him*. The thought sent color racing to her cheeks.

Inside the tent, May stirred from the rug. She sat up facing Sam who was sprawled happily on the ground.

"So, you said there is something you wanted to tell me?" Dana heard her ask. Her voice was barely audible over the light patter of raindrops on the canvas canopy, making Dana strain to hear.

"Yes, I did," Sam responded, sitting up to face her, looking uneasy. "It's something I need to show you." He pulled out a small electric lantern from a nearby nightstand, placing it on the ground between them. "Turn on the lamp."

She flicked the switch on the top.

Dana watched them from beneath her bush, wondering what the hell was going on. She leaned in closer to observe Sam; his eyes were half-closed and he swayed slightly, seemingly intoxicated as he stared at the absurdly intense brightness of his lamp.

"Sam?" May reached up to touch him, earning a weak groan. Dana watched him keenly. Every hair on her neck tingled in anticipation and wonder. May quickly turned off the light and tried again.

"Sam, are you okay?" She tapped him as she spoke. "Are you alright?" she repeated, leaning closer.

"Yeah, yeah I'm fine. It was just the lamp," he said, still a bit flustered as his eyes blinked open.

"Yeah?" May prompted.

"It affects my kind somehow. The way we react to it." He rubbed his eyes. "Like the way I was attracted to your lamp that night in the woods. It's why I can't really be out at night, when fluorescent lights come on, especially car headlights; it triggers almost like a deep hypnosis. It has killed more than one member of my family," he muttered in a low voice. Dana strained to listen. She watched his face with keen interest, trying to interpret the expression in his eyes and read the words off his lips.

"They hypnotize you even in human form?"

"Yes, I'm oddly attracted to lights, as you might have noticed," he explained. "For a moth, that's quite normal," he defended with a casual shrug. "The sun's light has no effect on me, thankfully, neither has the moon. They're celestials and are too far away I guess." He reached for May's hands as his voice lowered to a conspiratorial whisper. "Different colors have different affects, too . . . Red fire light ignites a passion in me and gets me really hot, orange heat lamps relax my mind, classic yellow lights dull my senses and ability to focus. What's really important, though, is if I'm exposed to pulsating green lights, like the ones that come out of the earth on my weekly . . . ritual. Those completely take over my mind; they can even make me transform into a moth off-schedule. I shouldn't be telling this to anyone," Dana heard him emphasize. "Though, since you already know most of the secrets, I thought you should know. Besides, I don't want any secrets between us, right?"

"No secrets between us," May echoed. "I'm glad you told me, Sam," she assured, resting her head on his chest, purring as he wrapped his arms around her. For what seemed like a long time, no one moved as the fire crackled underneath the canopy of trees.

This was a lot to digest. Dana was mesmerized, and could not completely believe her newly acquired information. She had spent more than a decade running, always silently hoping to find someone who could understand her. And here he was, the weird hobo from the woods, right under her nose the whole time. She was so close to him, but still so far away.

Dana's mind raced. She wanted to run out and let them know she knew, more than anything. It was all she could do to stay hidden even a minute longer! No, no she had to be smart; she couldn't waste this opportunity. That meant she couldn't risk letting them see her until she was completely certain. A snug spot in a niche beneath the roots of a huge oak tree offered her adequate shelter. There, Dana rested, looking up at the sky through the dense leafy canopy.

All she had left to do was wait a little longer. She needed to be patient.

* * *

May's sleep was restless, full of violent tosses and turns.

She woke up with an innate sensation that they were being watched. Something or someone was out there, somehow; she knew it. Every nerve in her body was tense, and a shiver ran up her spine. How could Sam sleep so soundly beside her with a wide grin stretched across his face? She ran her fingers through his dense brown hair and noted the silkiness of his two furry antennas. She now understood why he constantly wore that red beanie. The antennas seemed to be the only moth part of him constantly there, even when the rest of him was not transformed. Despite the heavy feeling in the air, she smiled fondly at him.

Maybe it was just paranoia; she couldn't bring herself to disturb him. Leaving him to his pleasant dreams, she stepped out of the tent, gathering a few branches for the fire and stopping beside the blackberry bush to stare into the vast darkness of the forest. Her intuition grew stronger, and she worried that whatever was out there wasn't friendly.

Sam stirred under the blanket, as if awoken by her absence. Barefoot and shirtless, he tracked May's short trail of footprints.

"May?" he called with sleepy eyes. "What are you doing outside?"

"There's something out there," she said with certainty, staring into the gloomy night. The feeling was eating away at her, hanging in the air, like a dark cloud looming over them.

"Of course, we're being watched," he said casually. "We're not the only creatures in these woods."

"This is different," she insisted, shaking her head stubbornly. "Something is out there, Sam. Can't you feel it?"

"Whatever is out there won't hurt us," he assured her. "I know these woods, May. There is no danger in this area." He extended a hand to her. "Come with me. It's like, three A.M., we should get inside." With one last suspicious glance in the darkness, she complied. Returning to the warmth of his arms, under their blankets where everything was wonderful, and where nothing could hurt her. Whatever evil was out there would likely vanish with the first rays of sunlight.

* * *

In the darkness, Dana curled inside her niche and drifted in and out of sleep.

She was always running in her dreams. Running from a hungry beast with a hundred faces, she *knew* that the monster intended to murder her. In the dream, sometimes the villain took her parents and her brother while she was helpless to stop it, but it always ended the same. She would run as fast as her legs could carry her until suddenly her foot got caught and she fell, too

105

weak to pull herself up again. All the while, the monstrous thing continue to rage and hone in on her until the moment of impact and WAKE UP!

It was perfectly normal for her to come out of sleep shivering. The dreams were vivid and too frequent to bear much longer. It had gotten to a point where she could barely even sleep, no matter how tired she was. She clamped her eyes tight to force the nightmares out of her thoughts. One day, she hoped to finally get rid of the last vestiges of distant memories, to somehow forget. What was worse was there was nobody she could tell. Until now, maybe. Tonight—for good or ill—she would face her demons.

She would tell someone.

She climbed out of her grassy alcove, her body numb with cold. A light dew had settled on her throughout the night, soaking through her clothes. It didn't matter, she could endure it.

Dana pulled the hood of her sweatshirt over her head and took off for the bright tent surrounding his cabin, trudging slowly on frozen feet. She stopped by the blackberry bush and peeked inside through the thorny foliage.

The young man stirred while May slept soundly beside him. From her position, she could only see a hand and a leg piercing through the thick blankets. He stirred, rising into a seated position, facing in her direction and making Dana jerk back in shock.

His eyes were wide open and staring blankly at her. She had never seen eyes like this before. Plate sized orbs of vivid gold that didn't blink and seemed to glow with their own light; it took a moment to even notice the pair of furry gray antenna poking through his thick brown hair. From his back, his miniature brown wings sprouted and grew into massive proportions before her very eyes.

It was true.

God help her it was true!

She felt as if she would faint, her own eyes nearly as wide in disbelief. Thankfully, he only pulled himself up and exited the tent, not noticing her. In a few moments, he rose by fluttering his wings and reached the tree tops. He beat them faster in the midnight air, while remaining motionless on the branch, as if calling out to something.

A smokey, teal green began to rise in a great circle that encapsulated them both, bleeding out of the earth up into the air, trailing the faintest bit toward him.

CHAPTER 14

O *ur father, who art in heaven,*
     Hallowed be thy name.
     Thy kingdom come.'

The voices filled the church and echoed off every wall, beam, and rafter, like the crash of distant waves on a rocky shore.

'Thy Will be done, on earth
As it is in Heaven.'

May stood straight at her seat in the front pews of the long hall, feeling lost in this crowd of worshippers.

She had always attended church with her parents, right up until the age of eight, when her mother had died. Her dad could hardly even be bothered to take her to school after that. Now, returning to the same Presbyterian Church where her mother had worshipped as a girl, she felt strangely unwelcome. The mystery of her mother's sudden flight from the town loomed over her mind with every polite conversation, but she couldn't trust anyone enough to talk about it. Repeatedly, all she could think about was her recent premarital sex, how if Mom and Dad were right, she was trending toward hell.

So, she kept to herself, as well as her misgivings, while putting on her most pious face.

'Give us this day our daily bread.

And forgive us our trespasses,

As we forgive those who trespass against us.'

She looked around the church and noted everyone's individual faces. She couldn't help noticing the disparity of ages among the congregation. More than two-thirds of the worshippers were elderly, the infirm, or young children. *Aunt Randa is right about one thing,* May couldn't help but think. *Young Americans hardly go to church anymore.* She looked at the presiding reverend, sitting pristinely between his two associates, an immensely cumbersome bible resting on his lap.

'And lead us not into temptation,

But deliver us from all evil.'

She looked at Aunt Randa standing beside her. Her face was heavily contorted into an enraptured grimace of fervent worship and supplication. She stared at the rafters like she could see through them to God's heavenly abode. Ed stood, looking dejected, in his Sunday clothes. His gray shirt was tucked into neatly ironed black trousers with a black tie and shoes to match. He complained like clockwork when his mother insisted they all attend church together, but in the end, he bent to her will every time.

He stood at the end of the bench next to Frank, who looked completely indifferent with a mild boredom on his face. He stared ahead with half closed eyes, trying to nap. He had not ever fought like his brother when Aunt Randa insisted they attend service together, but he clearly got no enjoyment from it.

Hell, he'd chugged at least three servings of whiskey before they left, and probably would have brought a bottle along if his mom had let him. She could see his face, and from the red flush on his cheeks to the slight droop of drool on his mouth, she could tell he was still feeling that booze.

For thine is the kingdom, the power and the glory,
Forever and ever, Amen.

The prayer ended and they settled into their seats while the reverend took to the podium to begin the Sunday sermon. As he started his long tirade, May drifted off in her own reveries about her own family. They had lived in Roxton Borough, which was a small suburb on the outskirts of Boston. Her father, George, was a mechanic at the now-abandoned Chevron assembly plant. Her mother, Helen, was the heart of the family, a tireless, doe-eyed beauty who miraculously juggled the daunting tasks of working at the neighborhood convenience store while caring for their home and infant daughter. She also kept May's father off his bottle often enough to take them rafting on Saturdays and to the local chapel on Sundays. For eight years, she had worked frantically, struggling to hold their hastily assembled family through the financial, emotional, and psychological rollercoaster of an officially unwed couple.

Until she had died, suddenly and abruptly. It had been a blood clot or something of the type. May barely remembered the details, but still, the loss had devastated her. It was years before she was able to accept the absence of her mother and move on. It broke her father. He had lost the love of his life, the mother of his child, his strong right arm, and his last hold on reality. He also lost interest in church, work, and even his eight-year-old daughter. He got drunk every night. May would complain or make a fuss sometimes, but that was quickly abandoned. She learned quickly that she was just another noise in his wine-soaked mind.

She became her father's caretaker and saw to all her own needs. He no longer had the ability or desire to raise his adolescent daughter. She had raised herself and done a good job of it, as far as she was concerned. Two years ago, she had graduated from college with a degree in nursing and hospital management. Not bad for the daughter of a drunk!

It was past time for her to leave the home, she then knew.

So here she was, in the town her mother grew up in, promised a free place to stay with her aunt. In a way, it made her feel close to her lost mother. She still grieved her loss, and it was painful to see the resemblance and kinship in Aunt Randa, the plump, middle-aged aunt beside her. Personality-wise they couldn't have been more different; her mother was warm, non-judgmental, full of love and devotion to her family.

May was lost, fully absorbed in her somber reflections for the duration of the sermon, jerking slightly when the crowd moved almost as one from the rows of benches after they were dismissed. This had been her first Sunday with the family at church, work giving a convenient excuse to miss all of the other invitations. Aunt Randa wanted to show off the latest addition to her family, and this weekend she finally got her way. May smiled her most pleasant smile as she was introduced to damn near everyone in town.

"Mrs. Baker," the reverend beamed as he approached. "How nice of you to grace us with your presence today." He was a short, thick, and balding man in his late forties, with a round face and no neck. A fat man that threatened to overflow his sky blue shirt and snap his suspenders. He had good manners at least, speaking with a gay and jolly tone.

"Reverend Gaius," Aunt Randa replied merrily. "Nice to see you, too. You know I've been quite busy of late, campaign stuff and all that."

"I see, I see," he said, in a tone that sounded like a scolding parent. "Oh, but I must thank you for your donation to the charity and Evangel Outreach Programs. People like you are the true pillars of our dear community!"

"It's always an honor to be of service to the church, Reverend," she beamed. "Some of us actually do care about the well-being of the less privileged, and other God's children in our midst, unlike some other so-called honorable members of the community."

"Grow some balls and call him out, Mom," Frank teased as he rolled his eyes. "You mean to say men like James Arthur."

"Yes, I did!" she admitted angrily. "That man, a self-proclaimed atheist. How can someone like that hope to represent this country with such godless inclination? Don't you agree, Reverend?"

The fat preacher nodded sagely.

"I'm sure the good Lord knows his true servants." Seemingly satisfied by the so-called response, she turned to May, standing forlorn by the side. The young woman felt herself tense.

"And this is my niece, May. She is my late sister, Helen's, only child."

"Hello, May," the reverend said, reaching out to shake her hand. "Welcome to our church. We're also a family, of a different sort . . .   And truly, I'm so sorry for what happened to your mother. Helen was a really special girl." His voice sounded oddly sad and genuinely full of grief, like it was more than a platitude. Still, May dared not speak up. He turned to the boys. "And how are you getting along with the little rogues?"

"With due respect, Rev, it's been many years since either of us were little," Frank quipped.

"Yeah, I can see that," the Reverend replied dryly.

The tension seemed to have spread to the entire family. May noticed Aunt Randa's nervous smile, Frank's cool glazed eyes, and the bulging vein on the reverend's forehead. Ed looked as angry as ever when he was spoken to.

"And what about you, son?" he asked. "What do you think of your new de facto sister?"

The younger twin remained silent throughout the entire exchange. Now, he stared evenly at the fat man, regarding him with cold gray eyes. He frowned harder as he spoke.

"What I think is of little consequence to you and your church, sir," he offered in a dead, flat tone.

"Hah!" Aunt Randa laughed nervously. "Kids? You know I love them. I'm so sorry about that. I'll see you about the ecclesiastical bulletin when I return from Mission Hill. Happy Sunday, Reverend!" she called rapidly, turning to flee with short, hurried steps, leaving May alone with the holy man.

She turned to the preacher and searched for words to say while plotting her own escape.

"May God guide you, child," he said, patting her shoulder. "It is a strange home you have come to," he added before walking away, leaving May at the empty podium, feeling oddly isolated.

She caught up with the Bakers in the car while Aunt Randa waited in her black sedan. She settled in the back seat with Ed while her aunt raged.

"You spoiled little shit!" she fumed. "What did you think you were doing, talking to the reverend like that? Can't you see how bad that makes us look?"

"I don't care how that made us look," he spat back, words slow, exaggerated. "Look Mom, you can pretend about who you are to everybody but don't ask the same of me. I didn't want to come." Aunt Randa remained silent, stricken by his words too much to conjure a reply. A few tense seconds passed, then she started the car instead.

"I would pray for your soul, Ed," Frank jested from the front seat. "But I don't remember all the words for that. Besides, I doubt there's much of anything left to save in us," he joked.

As the car turned out of the church driveway, May couldn't help but recall the reverend's last words to her. She wondered how long she could remain lucid in this strange, toxic family. Who could be saved?

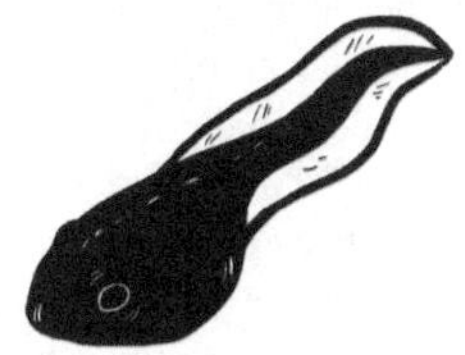

CHAPTER 15

S am led May blindly through the rough footing of the forest floor.

With her eyes covered by her thick wool scarf, her world shrank down to the sounds of her ears and the smells drifting through the air. She smelled wet earth, rot, pungent berries, and sweet flowers all combined on the cool breeze. She heard the slight rustling of leaves as the wind glided through the trees, as well as the sparrows singing their songs in the treetops with the mockingbirds, all muffled by the roar of the stream.

"Aren't we there yet?" she complained. "I've been stumbling blindly for like an hour now."

"Don't exaggerate, May," he replied from directly before her. "It's been barely ten minutes." He led her by the hand toward the ever-increasing rumble of the river. "Careful, careful. Watch your step," he teased.

"This better not be a prank, Sam," she said, blindly groping for support as she stumbled on. "It better be worth it!"

She staggered after him, holding tightly to his hands until the soft grassy ground under her feet gave way to a sleek rocky surface washed by the spray from the bloated stream.

"Here we are," he said, finally letting go of her hand and easing the makeshift blindfold off her eyes.

May blinked twice as her eyes adjusted to the sudden bright glare. The sun shone on her face with golden rays; the sky was an array of bright shades of blue, turning a deeper cobalt and then a darker shade of indigo as it rose from the western horizon, still shrouded in the gloomy shades of predawn.

The forest awakened before her eyes, clothed in all shades of green, brown, and autumn gold. The large broadleaves and smaller rowans around them still held the colors of fall. Through the dense leafy canopy, she saw the twinkling sheen of the clear sapphire stream. It twinkled in the morning light as it meandered around and through the soft ground, crags, and subterranean caves. The river flowed before them and ended abruptly in a sixty-foot drop to a rocky pool below.

May stood upon the edge of the world, gazing at one of the most astonishing sunrises of her life.

The air was fresh, and her hair was blowing behind her like a black tassel banner. She turned to him, barely able to contain her wide and growing smile. Sam smiled, too. In the sun, his face glistened and his brown eyes were vibrant. He knew she would like it, and she did—doubly so because he was with her.

"So?" he asked, cocking his head to the side. "Was it worth it?"

She smiled and turned away from him, playfully refusing to give him the satisfaction.

"Well, it's not the worst sight I've seen today," she said, gazing back at the sensually intoxicating view. "It's not the best either," she teased him with a sidelong smirk.

"Oh wow!" he said, stepping up to wrap his hands around her waist. "So that means I'm the best sight you've seen today?"

"Aren't you such a modest fellow?" she mocked.

"Well, what can I say?" he returned. "When you're dating the hottest girl in town, a certain measure of arrogance is in order."

"Is that what we're doing, dating?" she asked, smiling her secret smile. "So, I'm your girlfriend? When did that happen?"

"I don't know, myself," he admitted. "Though that seems like the most likely reason why we're cuddled against each other on a cliff, watching this magical sunrise together."

"Maybe I'm only playing you." She whipped up her head defiantly, playful. "Ever thought of that?"

"I am now, thanks to you," he replied, sounding irritated. "You could be playing me, I know that. Maybe you're the new county sex doll, just an apprentice to Dana, tearing your way across town."

"What?" she said, aghast. "That's unfair. Dana's a bit flirty, but she's not a slut or anything!"

"Ha, if you say so," he quipped.

"And how would you know?" she asked, her voice growing a slight edge now. "Have you been . . .?"

"Can we not talk about your friend now?" he asked, cutting her off. "It'll just ruin the moment."

"Whatever," she yielded, settling back into an uneasy silence. She hadn't meant to quarrel, but she still felt unsure about their relationship. There were times when she feared this meant more to her than it did to him, and the insecurity bothered her far more than she had ever expressed. The silence chafed her, and she silently cursed herself for being needy. He hadn't given her any reason to doubt him.

"You said your hometown is not far from here," she said, trying to start another conversation, a *safer* conversation.

"Yeah, a few miles south," he said, sounding rather sullen. "That way," he added, pointing toward a low ridge covered with pines, sentinels, and other giant conifers. "Just beyond those trees is the small town of Westbrook and my family, my friends, and most of my kind."

"Do you miss them?" she asked. "Your family and the others like you?"

"It's not like I don't visit," he replied, chuckling lightly. "Sometimes I fly down there, or just hitchhike, help my father tend the apple orchards and have some of my mother's delicious tarts." He took a lungful of air and smiled wistfully. "The smell of baking bread on Sunday morning, or steaming hot mushroom broth on cold winter nights. The smell of the gold-leafed rowans in autumn . . . That's home, in my brain."

He turned away and walked upstream, as if he was going to trek down there this instant. He started down the gentle slope of the ridge and found his way around the cliff to the pool below. She heard the longing in his voice, the affection. It was so unlike how she felt whenever she had to speak about her mother and their little home in Roxton Borough.

"It sounds like a wonderful place, Sam." she offered, trying to catch up to him. "But if you were so happy back there, why leave?" She couldn't even imagine why anyone would abandon such a beautiful life of love and companionship for one of such loneliness and caution.

"I could tell you that I left because I had to find you," he chuckled dryly. "Or that I left to find true love at least, but you're far too smart to believe that, right?"

"Yeah," she admitted. "That'd be too cheesy, even for you."

"Well, the truth is cheesy sometimes," he said. "I left because of the trees. I loved walking in the woods, the sound of wildlife, foraging, nature. Plus, it's real nice almost never having to worry about those confusing bright lights." He gave a casual shrug. "So, one day I left my home, my friends, and family to begin my exciting life as a forest hermit."

There was no regret in his tone, and the yearning in his voice subsided by the end. He seemed back to normal, if a little embarrassed. After a short silence, she asked her question.

"And so far?"

"Well, you know, it's worked out pretty great for me so far," he commented, wrapping his hands around her waist slowly as she caught up with him, staring down at her with a loving look. She tried to fight back her smile but failed. She was anxious. Sam was clearly head over heels into her, and she felt the same, but how would she reconcile this forbidden affair with her strange family? If her aunt couldn't tolerate her son dating a singer, she would go ballistic to hear about some hermit in her home. Someone was bound to get hurt.

Baker people never seemed to be happy in love.

"But what if this . . . this . . ." she stammered uncertainly. "I come from a strange family, Sam,"

"Stranger than mine?" he chuckled, arching a brow.

"No, not like that," she admitted. "But . . . I don't know, I worry about the future,"

"We'll figure it out," he assured, gripping her hand, and looking into her eyes with that warm smile. "Come on, let's go swimming!" he declared, rushing off further from the waterfall and its deceptively dangerous tide, leading them back to the pool below. He knew the safe spots to swim.

The water was pleasantly cool on his skin as he broke through the surface of the pond, plunging into the warmer waters below. He swam toward the sandy beach by the pool, kicking through the water with strong athletic legs. To his mother's dismay, he had learned to hold his breath underwater for far longer than his kind and even most humans. Moths did not swim or fly in the rain, she was always quick to remind him. Wet wings are the bane of insects and insect-like people.

But this moth swam and strongly at that. Why not? He didn't consider himself half man or feel like he was inferior to other people; he would claim every enjoyment due to the denizens of the human world possible. He swam, he rode, he danced, and now he had carnal knowledge of a most amazing human woman. What more could a moth freak like him ask for?

He broke the surface of the water, his prize clutched tightly in one hand as he took a mighty lungful of air. The warm stormy water in the pool fell sixty feet off the edge of the cliff with a loud crash that churned the water like bubbles in a soda can. Not to mention the tingly vibrations it caused through the pond.

He swam through the strong current where May knelt over the high rocky bank, playing with newly hatched tadpoles and fingerlings in the shallow water. She had refused to join him in the deep water, insisting it was too early in the day for drowning. Besides, this was pretty entertaining, too.

"I once knew a girl who feared the water so much, she never bathed," he announced as he waded through the knee-deep water. "She was four, and my niece, and grew out of it, but still. Made for a harrowing month," he elaborated, making her look of mild interest fall away.

He made a silly face at her.

"And here's what the little moth says to the little human girl." He gently petted his crotch. "Leave the little fingerlings and come play with the big fish." He watched her eyes flicker down to his crotch and flash away, abashed. His light shorts were soaked from his swim and clung tightly to his skin, which exposed every little harness of his cock, not to mention his toned thighs. She picked up a little rock and aimed for his head.

"Go away with your little sardine," she retorted playfully. "I'll have myself a nice fat trout or salmon. You can take your little fish to your friend, *Dana*. Since you seem to know what she likes."

"Tsk, jealousy, it'll become you, May," he teased, even as he sighed internally. *This girl never forgets things in a hurry.* "But you do me great wrong, miss, for what man would seek out a candle when the sun still shines," he recalled the line from a half-remembered movie from his childhood, but he could see it made her smile.

"Mister Samwell," she said, surprised. "I never would have taken you for a poet."

"You never would," he agreed, trying to sound like her purported poet. "But take my hand, my lady, and I will be whatever you need me to be, so I swear." With a callow grin, he extended his prize to her—a sapphire blue shell crusted with bright red spots.

"Oh Sam, you sweet little fish!" she cooed as he brought it closer. "Such cuteness will get you anything."

"Anything?" he asked, arching an eyebrow.

"You bet," she said, carefully taking the shell from his palm and admiring it.

He grabbed her free hand and pulled her into the stream. He heard her quick gasp before her body slapped the water with a soft splash. She shrieked and squealed as she thrashed in the waist-deep water before realizing she could stand. When she finally found her footing, she attempted to climb out, only for Sam to grab her again, raise her into the air, and playfully swing her around before slamming her back into the water.

She screamed while flailing and lightly beating on him wherever she could reach. Soon she found her footing again, and he knocked her back into the water, this time with a casual push, far from his full strength. Before long, they were both locked in a wet grapple, wrestling in the pristine waist-high water. Her panicked screams turned into breathless laughter as it went on.

By the time they grew tired and dragged themselves aground, the sun was high, shining brightly in the sky for once. It was a welcomed break in the otherwise so gloomy weather, especially since they were both soaked to the bone. He climbed onto the rocky bank and helped her up. Her clothes dripped with water and clung tightly to her nubile body.

"Is this your little trick to get me out of my clothes?" she asked, thrashing her arms and spraying water everywhere. Sam hadn't exactly had that in mind, but he was not about to miss an opportunity. "Maybe," he offered coyly. "Did it work?"

"More than you know, you little sneak," she growled, slipping off her shirt. "I hope you're prepared for what's coming," she breathed out. Her raunchy behavior excited him. During their little struggle in the shallows, he touched her body in ways that left him half hard already. He was pleased to see it wasn't one-sided.

She fixed him with an incredibly sexy stare.

"Your clothes make me uncomfortable. Take `em off."

He rushed to obey and ripped off his own wet shirt and shorts in a hasty fashion that seemed to spur his urge, revealing every inch of his damp, naked body. From his wide shoulders to his small belly, his muscled limbs and bright, eager eyes. Now excited, he remembered her sensual striptease in their canvas tent nights ago, and the delightful events that followed.

The sun burned hot on them. She slipped off her own water-dripping clothes and locked him in a fiery kiss as she guided him to a softer spot of grass beneath the whitewood tree. They broke off after a few seconds, both panting hard, too excited to draw out the foreplay much longer. He reached down and tried slipping a hand to her wet womanhood, but she slapped it away.

"No," she demanded, shaking her head. "It's my turn today." With the remark, she took to her knees like a penitent sinner.

She grabbed hold of either side of his hips, bracing herself as she stared at his manhood. His cock dangled long and stiff between his legs, pointing at her face imposingly. She looked up at him, guileless green eyes full of anxiety. It was obvious she had never done what she was about to, and that made Sam unsure.

"Seems like there's trout on the menu after all," she joked, trying to ease her own tension even as her voice cracked. He chuckled nervously, his body still tight and tense as his erect member hung dauntingly an inch from her beautiful, full lips.

She rubbed on it, slowly running her hand along the long, throbbing shaft, squeezing gently as she ran over the enlarged head. The moisture on their bodies eased the friction along the length like a natural lubricant. Her hands were soft and gentle as she rubbed on him, making him sigh in relief. She deftly increased the pace and pressure of her strokes, making him moan softly as his heart rate grew wild.

After a minute or so, she tried her mouth, squeezing the head through her parted lips. He jerked slightly in pain when her teeth scraped his skin, causing her to look up in alarm at his face, fearing she had ruined things. Sam's smile melted away her anxieties, but even so, he patted her head and encouraged her to carry on.

She parted her lips, opened her mouth wide and slid her tongue down the bottom side of the shaft to ensure her teeth came nowhere close. It felt awkward at first, a sloppy attempt at best, but she was a fast learner. Before long, she mastered the rhythm, sliding along half the length of his musky cock with wet lips while her hand curled around the base.

It was such a unique flavor, not entirely pleasant, but so utterly *masculine.*

May felt herself getting lost in it.

He shuddered from the wetness of her mouth. It was warm, and the gentle squeeze of her tongue left him dazed. Sam didn't know what he'd possibly done to deserve such bliss, or how long he would be able to last under it. Considering her inexperience, he considered it best not to fight his release. All he felt was the rising tension in his groin and the intense throbbing of his dick. He felt himself twitch as his member became more agitated, more desperate for release.

She must have felt it too because she pulled back just in time to avoid his enormous eruption. Even to her, it was obvious what the sudden spasming and throbbing and swelling of the dick in her mouth meant. His breath quivered as he gasped in the recoil of his explosive climax, releasing only inches away from her face. Sam eased himself down the tree trunk he had been leaning against until he was seated on the ground, feeling completely languid from the impact of the most incredible blowjob of his life.

He could still see her through his half-closed eyes, crouched astride his legs, her hands running slowly over his hips and the hard muscles of his thighs. She wasn't done with him, yet. Sam smiled again.

May leaned in to kiss his chest, his neck, and every crevice of his chiseled pecks. He reached out a hand to cup her breast and feel the warm softness while she worked, eager to give her some pleasure back for her trouble. When she reached down to rub his cock again, she was shocked to find him hard as stone again already. She stroked his erect member, her soft hands gliding along the spittle-soaked shaft.

The young woman straddled him and gently lowered her body on his erect cock. He could feel her envelop him, his throbbing manhood bathing in the warm, soppy caress of her pussy. His body entering hers, inhabiting it, connecting with it. It was absolutely divine.

That was before she even began moving. The pace was gentle but switched speeds often, her hips rocking back and forth in an intense swaying dance. He rubbed her soft skin, held her hips with one arm and stroked her hair with the other, frantically searching for purchase as she rocked his world. His senses were escalating into another explosive climax.

May jerked from the force of his second orgasm. Her body trembled from the feeling of her own imminent peak. It washed over her as he came, a cascade of quivering limbs and trembling thighs as his hot cum filled her again. They spent a good moment just breathing in silence. Then Sam wrapped his strong arms around May as they nestled in the shade of the large whitewood. Their shaky breaths mingled, and both were completely, undeniably satisfied.

CHAPTER 16

He held an umbrella steadily above her head as they hurried.

They ran in sprints through the parking lot to the front door of the MCMC. Out of breath and quite wet. Her loose gray shirt and jean trousers clung to her wet skin.

Tony was in far worse shape; if May was wet, he was *drenched*. By choosing to hold the umbrella above her head and leaving himself open to the pouring rain, he'd volunteered himself for such fate. His clothes dripped puddles into his boots and left pools on the floor. The bulky man shivered violently as he shook the last drops of water from the umbrella.

She felt an odd sympathy for him, almost like a pang of guilt. He noticed her stranded at the bus station with a group of commuters that morning, having been unable to find a ride to work. The open pavilion at the station barely kept the rain out.

Every gust of wind sent more lashing into their faces. Just then, he drove by in his truck, parked by the road, and ran a couple of yards out through the pouring rain to offer her a ride.

They were cold and shivering, but at least she had finally gotten to work, while he was cold and still miles away from his intended destination. May almost felt bad. Sure he was imposing, and he'd scared her more then a little, but perhaps her fear was unwarranted. He hadn't made any more advances since that last time in the clinic, including today. But she had promised herself not to be alone with him again, and her intuition still indicated that something wasn't quite right. But she did not feel like she had much choice if she were to get to work in time. Seeing him shivering and dripping with water, looking like a drowned rat, she couldn't help but letting her empathic side win.

"Come on in and dry up," she finally suggested. "You're gonna catch a cold."

"I don't know about catching a cold," he said through clattering teeth, "but I'm darn sure the cold's caught me." Still, he followed her into the nurses' locker room, trudging along on heavy soaked boots and leaving a trail of mud puddles for each step.

The locker room was blessedly warm. She quickly rubbed her own damp skin with a towel and offered him one as well. They both tried to dry while she peeled off the rain sodden layers of her clothes to collect in a heap of wet fabrics beside her locker.

May was slipping off her shirt when she felt his stare from behind her. Turning around she found him gazing at her with lips slightly parted, his narrow dark eyes crawling over every inch of her body. May shivered again. Then for a moment, she froze under the intensity of the stare. She could see what he intended in his jet-black eyes. For a moment, she stared at them, finding herself pulled deep into his wild gaze.

Whatever was going on behind those black eyes was dangerous and forbidden in all senses. And she found herself feeling both curious and alarmed. It was like that animalistic hungry energy in his eyes hypnotized her. She could sense the danger, but had a hard time fighting it.

"Umm, hello?" she finally managed to call, snapping him from whatever reverie he was in. "Do you mind? I'm gonna change here; you can use the toilet or wait outside," she insisted.

A crooked grin appeared on his face, his eyes still scanning her body. The wet clothes plastered against her body, and her white shirt, slightly transparent from the water, revealed her perky breasts and erect nipples through the fabric from the cold.

He slowly stepped toward her and she could hear his breath quickening. She backed up until her back suddenly hit the lockers. She could clearly see the bulge under his wet trousers before he almost pinned her against the cold metal locker door.

"Alright, I'll wait outside," he declared, before turning around.

After a few moments, she turned back to her clothes, fighting the color rising up to her cheeks. He still made her uncomfortable, the way he leered at her, unashamed to show his interest. It always made her blush to think about it, and she often found herself holding her breath around him.

She fought the strange sensation.

He is rough and uncouth, she tried to tell herself. *Besides, he is Dana's fling. Maybe not just Dana's, even. He is the same for many other girls in this town. What girl wouldn't want a piece of that man's meat?*

The drenched woman slammed hard on that train of thought. She had Sam now. Sure, Tony was strangely exciting, but that only shamed her; she had a great man who treated her right and made her happy. *Sammy is much better than this lusty liver,* she thought, realizing it wasn't Tony she craved, it was the untamed and absolute passion she had seen in his eyes.

She picked up her phone to call Sam before abandoning her privacy. Her heart raced at the prospect of another meeting. It'd been two days since their so-called date at the waterfall, and she already missed him sorely. She wondered how she got so attached.

"Hello," his voice came from the other end of the line. "Good morning, babe,"

"Hey Sam," she replied, trying to keep her voice even and unperturbed. "What's up?"

"Umm . . . The ceiling?" he joked.

"Ha-ha," she replied dryly. That line was old, but it still made her smile.

"Aren't you tired?" he asked randomly.

"What? What are you talking about?"

"You should be tired," he replied. "The way you've been running through my mind all morning."

She laughed. He had a way of calming her nerves with his cheesy remarks. She was suddenly reminded of what she liked about him. That aura, the way everything about him seemed to calm her.

"You know, you really need to work on your pick-up lines, Sam," she threw back at him. "Maybe something smarter or, at least, more current; these ones are from the Stone Age."

"I only use them because you laugh," he defended. "Besides, I am a caveman, don't forget. I don't do smart or modern things. I like stream and tree and fire," he said with a brutish grunt.

She laughed again, her awkward and alarming moment with Tony totally forgotten. Just then, Dana walked into the room, her cloth bag slung across her shoulder. She glanced over at a partially unclad May laughing by the locker and shook her head, obviously amused by the sight.

"Well, Mister Caveman, put your cave-in order," May suggested. "You're mate is coming over tonight."

"Are you sure? It's only been two days," he teased

"I know," she admitted, somewhat upset at his reluctance. "I just miss you, that's all,"

"I see," he deviously replied. "Craving some more . . . *trout,* are we? Well, come on by, bring friends, there's enough trout for everyone!"

She scoffed.

"You wish, little sardine boy,"

"So . . . meet at my house?" he asked.

"Unless you have a five-star resort somewhere in those woods."

"That, I do not. Ah, a car's stopping, I gotta go," he replied. "Talk to you soon."

"Bye!"

CHAPTER 17

Rain fell endlessly from a dark and cloudy evening sky. The next morning, the clouds were still there. A faint hint of light traveled westward in the sky. The clouds wept over her, pouring relentless torrents that formed an unbroken curtain of water connecting earth and sky. Even under the thick canopy of Woods End's trees, the water came down earnestly. It drummed heavily on May's umbrella, turning the soft ground into a quagmire of perilously soft sand and treacherous little mudflats.

Even the forest life had vanished. She heard no birds or any miscellaneous critters. The loud sound of the thunder drowned out everything else. Or they were hiding from the elements like *intelligent* life forms. She struggled through the gloom while navigating through bush and wet underbrush, around little ravines caused by the heavy rain with her lamp held tight in one hand, her umbrella in the other, and her large backpack bouncing on her back.

Night had fallen on the world, and the rain still had not ebbed. When she got to the little grove beside the swollen stream, she cut through the thick watery curtain. She saw the white canvas tent hanging from the trees and the faint glow of the fire burning within the structure proper. She quickened her pace, eager for the warmth from the fire on her cold skin.

Eager for Sam.

Inside the cabin was already significantly warmer, and she was happy to be out of the rain. She rushed to reseal the doorway and blow the dying embers of the fire back to life. As the smoke began trailing more steadily up the chimney, she realized the obvious oddity in their little pavilion; Sam wasn't there.

She looked around and behind the tent outside, under the heap of blankets in the corner, and underneath the blackberry bush, but he still remained elusive. May began to worry he wasn't just playing with her. Where could he have gone in this storm?

"Sam! Sam!" she cried out futilely. The storm drowned her words out with ease. "Sam! Sam! Where are you?!"

She hollered until her throat was sore, but he still had not put up an appearance. Her fears grew by the minute. This wasn't like him. He wouldn't just leave, at least *not of his own free will.* A voice echoed in her head. *Unless, it was something else that made him leave . . .* The thought scared May, and she grew restless waiting. She continued to search the camp for footprints or tracks. Though even she realized if there had been any trace to follow, the rain would have long washed them away.

So instead, she circled the camp, calling for him in the nearby trees in every direction. Her throat grew hoarser without success. Every time she tried to call his cellphone, it went straight to voicemail.

"Sam, I know you're out here. How else can you explain the fire?" The woods suddenly grew forebodingly still as an eerie silence answered her mumbled question. She remembered the uneasy feeling of being watched all too well; something was terribly wrong.

Rain sodden and frustrated, she returned to the little cottage. She changed into dry clothes and huddled to warm herself by the fire. Her boyfriend had apparently gathered some berries that she helped herself to. Settled in, she tried to distract her dark thoughts with a book, but her thoughts were just too heavy. *He would come back during the night,* she assured herself; it was the only thought that finally allowed her to fall sleep.

Almost immediately, she was transferred into a horrifying nightmare. A faceless monster came roaring through a terrible storm, scooping up Sam just before she reached him and hauling him away into the black.

She woke stiff and sore with cold. Early rays of sunlight shot diagonally through the clouds and foliage to erase the last vestiges of her dark dream. The leaves were still leaking water, and only a few of the birds deemed it safe to emerge from their hidey holes.

Her Sam was nowhere to be found.

He had not come home in the night.

***

The dawn was bright and sunny with isolated clouds in the sky, warming up the last traces of the night's chill. One of the few nice days she'd seen in this godforsaken town. It was the type of morning that promised a day of sunbathing, lunchtime picnics, and other outdoor frolics she'd grown to love.

May was in no mood to frolic. Her own dark cloud followed her to work that day. The rain of dreaded news seemed imminent as she listened for any talk of a mysterious disappearance from any of the staff or patients. Or worse, any talk of a body. After calling Sam multiple times with no answer, she feared the worst. Even her texts continued to go unreturned.

Dana noticed her gloom.

"Someone's having a bad day," Dana remarked while taking a seat beside her on the counter. "You look like someone just ate your boyfriend, haha." There was something wrong in her laugh. Or the joke just cut too close to the mark. She whirled to face Dana, voice demanding.

"What's that supposed to mean? Do you know something about Sam?"

"About what?" Dana asked, flustered by May's intensity.

"You just asked if someone ate my boyfriend," she insisted, grabbing her by the shoulders. Dana appeared bemused by her reaction, blinking a few times and holding her smile. Laughing even before she replied, sounding only slightly unnerved.

"Hey, chill out," she replied, pulling away slowly. "I was only joking. You know, him being a 'trout' and all?"

"Oh," she lapsed back into her depressed silence.

'Did something happen to him?" Dana inquired, a bit concerned now. "Did he . . . stand you up or something?"

"It's nothing," May replied, unwilling to divulge any more information till she was sure what had happened last night. Dana pressed May harder when her phone rang and rescued her. She snatched the cellphone from the desk like a junky and ran to a secluded corner of the room. It was Sam calling. She clicked to answer. "Hello?" she whispered into the phone, holding her breath and listening to the radio silence.

"Hello," the voice on the other end was strained and hushed, but she couldn't miss the unmistakable slur and drawl of his accent.

"Sam?" she asked, still frightened. "Sam, are you alright? What happened?"

"Yeah, I'm alright," he replied. His voice growing stronger. "I just . . . woke up and saw your texts. Is everything okay?"

"You *just* woke up?" she asked, completely befuddled, her mind still foggy with relief. "You worried me last night. I thought something bad happened to you!"

"Something bad?" he echoed. "Why would you think that?"

"Well, you weren't at home; you didn't come back all night!" she said. Her mind was a rattled mess. Then, it quickly dawned on her, and apprehension turned to anger. "You weren't at home," she repeated darkly. "You left me there, alone in the woods, and you don't want to tell me where you were?"

"I was there last night!" he rebutted. "I was right by my home and . . . fuck, May, I must have seen a light! I was conked out or hypnotized or something, the whole evening's a blur. I must have passed out staring at it."

"So, what happened then, what light could it have been?" she asked, not entirely dropping her guard.

"I don't know," he replied. "I just woke up this morning in the forest. I feel weird, my head hurts, but I don't remember much. I think I saw a bright yellow light and walked toward it, thinking it was your lamp. Maybe?"

"Sam?"

"Yeah?"

"Were you drinking?" she asked flatly.

"No," he winced. "I don't ever drink, believe me,"

"I don't know what to believe anymore," she said. "All I know is that I braved the rain to meet my boyfriend and got stood up."

They fell silent for a moment. The scary new possibility lingering in her mind. *What if he was with someone else that night?* He was reluctant when she asked to meet. Suddenly she was afraid. *What if I'm not enough? What if he's bored? Am I that inadequate?*

"Sam," she continued as the silence lingered.

"Yeah?"

"You wouldn't lie to me, would you?"

"Never," he insisted.

". . . Okay. I believe you," she proclaimed softly. "But just know I'm not gonna put up with anything like that. Don't betray me, okay? I couldn't take it if you ever did."

"I promise, May," his voice solemn. "I swear on my life, my mother's, and all else I hold dear."

She forgave him, even if he never really asked her for forgiveness. Even if the anger was genuinely misplaced, which it in fact was, as the young man was completely honest. It didn't matter in the moment to her, she hated being mad at him. The thought of losing him scared her more than she thought possible.

They made up and promised to be true to the end. He committed to another date in the woods ASAP to make it up to her, and she happily accepted. They made it through their first fight, she realized with some affection.

Look at me, handling relationships like a real grownup!

She chuckled to herself at the thought.

CHAPTER 18

The light rain drizzled steadily from a gray overcast sky. The soft drops were cold to the touch, and the brisk wind blew with a chill that heralded a fast-approaching winter. As May trudged miserably along the rutted track, the wind grew colder; the closer she got to the Baker Manor the worse it seemed. The wind bit through her rain-sodden clothes. Still, she felt no need to hurry or get out of the freezing elements. The clear, tasteless water running down her hair and face washed off the salty water of her tears. The gentle raindrops tapped lightly on her shoulder, which she found oddly comforting. Besides, she didn't exactly relish the thought of reaching home and being alone in her room. She just didn't have any better idea of what to do.

Nothing interested her anymore.

The first guy she had ever felt comfortable around was ghosting her. He had shown her what it meant to be loved and how it felt to be a woman. Then, he showed her the feeling of betrayal. Not only had he stood her up for the second consecutive night, this time someone answered his phone. Another woman, who told her he was indisposed and hung up in a hurry.

The memory was too fresh and the pain still raw. It did not feel like how she'd imagine heartbreak, not the kind they spoke of in movies or sad songs. This agony was physical, intense, and gut-wrenching. Her chest was tight as if actual daggers pierced her heart. It was all she could do not to double over on the muddy road and cry to her heart's content.

She had thrown his stupid beanie cap in the mud, which she still had from their first night together in the woods. May couldn't even fathom keeping it around while it reminded her of all the things she wanted to forget. Would he ever come back for it?

She finally stumbled into the Baker Manor's yard. Aunt Randa's black sedan was parked in front of the house between Frank's blue Ford and Ed's red Rover. Two other cars were parked in the driveway as well, a navy blue Jeep and a soot-colored vintage Cadillac. She recognized one by the sheriff's tags on it, the other was probably one of her aunt's numerous political associates.

She made her way around the cars and crept through the back door in hopes of avoiding the visitors and whatever chaos was happening in the house. Entering through the laundry door at the back, she almost bumped into the older maid, Maggie, who was hard at work. The sight only hastened her desire to escape upstairs, still, she greeted her.

"Oh, sorry,"

"May."

"I'm sorry," May muttered again, turning her face away in haste to get away. "I didn't see you there."

"I know," the woman assured, looking her over. "But I see you dear, and you look a proper mess."

May flushed miserably. She didn't need a mirror to know what she looked like. The rain had soddened her hair, which was plastered limply over her face. Her eyes were bloodshot and swollen from hours of crying her way home, along with a chapped nose from the constant wiping. Her clothes were filthy, hanging heavy from her body while still dripping water on the wooden floor.

To say nothing of the mud.

"Are you alright, dear?" the woman inquired, her brown eyes crinkling in mild concern.

God, even those reminded her of Sam, the brown eyes.

"Yes, I . . . umm . . ." May stammered and tried to explain why she was in the shape she was, but where would she even begin? She could try and start from the previous night in the woods, or Sam's blatant denial? Or the strangely familiar woman on the phone. The thoughts brought memories crashing back and made her relive them in her mind. Her chest heaved heavily as tears brewed anew behind her eyes.

"Oh my, never mind now," the woman waved off, obviously perceiving her unease. "I'm guessing it's nothing a hot bath and a good meal won't fix, or at least improve." She wiped her hands on her apron and reached to feel May's face with her palm. "You're so cold; bathe first, then come down to the dining room, I'll have something waiting for you." She turned away, disappearing back into the kitchen.

May couldn't even respond before meandering up to her room and shutting the door behind her. She stripped naked, leaving a giant clump of wet, muddy clothes on the floor. The clean sheets felt good on her bare skin as she curled up and huddled under her blankets, trying to hide in sleep. It was so unfair. Why was she the only one in pain? Why did he get to be happy with his whore while she felt like she was going to die from heartache? She remembered his cold, dead stare without blinking an eye. Her mind raced, thinking he was no doubt with her right now, probably eating her out, kissing, fucking, swimming, laughing, who knew!

Who was the woman? Was she a boyfriend thief or merely another victim?

Does he take her to our little glade with all the beautiful flowers? Did he take her to the grove or show her our waterfall?

May let out a silent scream and threw off her blankets. She promised herself never to curl up and cry herself to sleep again. She stumbled from the bed and shuffled lifelessly into the bathroom. She turned the handle on the faucet and filled the bathtub with steaming hot water.

The water was almost unbearably hot, but she immersed herself anyway. She let out a little yelp and willed herself to bask in the heat, which pervaded her body. It gave her mind focus, clarity, strength as it chased the cold from her bones and blanketed the other thoughts she wanted to avoid. The dirt from her skin came off in brown crusts and flakes. She scrubbed her body fiercely until her skin was pink and tender. She washed her hair with the fancy shampoo and conditioner she had stolen from her aunt, making it a joy to comb out the tangles.

It was over half an hour later when she found her way to the dining room. The ten-seater hardwood table was filled, giving her pause. Typically, there were never more than five occupants when they gathered for the regular family supper. This particular evening, there were nine sitting around Maggie's sumptuously prepared meal.

Aunt Randa sat at the head of the table with Ed and Frank on her flanks. Beside Frank was Captain Marcus, the county sheriff, a grizzled older man with a hairless head and a huge gray mustache. His eyes were half-closed with his mouth drooping open, looking half asleep. Next from the sheriff was a huge, balding man in a stained white shirt and coat. He attacked a greasy wing of crisp brown capon. Beside him, looking forlorn, was a pinched-face woman who looked to be his wife. Across from *them*, with his back to her, was a slim, sinewy man in a gray blazer suit and small bowl hat. The woman next to him was dressed in a long-sleeved dress of jade-colored wool.

May felt severely underdressed in her pajama pants.

At the other end of the table sat the outgoing county mayor. He was a diminutive man with close-cropped receding hair and shrewd black eyes. He sat silently at the table with his eyes even and impassive while the others chattered noisily amongst themselves. May took the final free seat between Ed and the slim man in the gray blazer. Thankfully, no one paid her any mind. They seemed to have more urgent discussions. She was grateful for that at least, and wasted no time on small talk or empty curtsies.

"I hear he's even promised to set up a new lumber mill in Wood's End," the slim man said with a soft, barely audible voice.

"That's my campaign promise," Aunt Randa complained. "More lumber means more taxes, that thieving bastard," she spat.

"Except he's not planning to tax them," Slim replied back.

"What?" Aunt Randa seemed pleasantly surprised. "How then does he plan to curtail their excessive tree felling?"

"I think he plans to hand over the forest reserve to Arthrost. His family owns the Luxury Resort Company," the woman in the green dress said with a sad laugh.

"Personally, I'd advocate a nice little hunt to clear those woods," the grizzled sheriff finally opened his eyes to say. "Years now we've been receiving reports of strange fires, weird green lights, and other signs of squatting."

May almost choked on her fruit salad. *Sam.* Suddenly, the conversation piqued her interest. She could only imagine what a patrol squad or a hunting party would do if they happened to find him turned, but she was past caring. Deep down, she hoped the police caught him along with whatever girl he'd tricked into bed.

"I'm telling you, it's a witch!" her aunt assured. "Witches *are* real as the good book says; hell, some of these kids these days *admit* to it. Though this one is dangerous, clearly has some dark power if they are doing rituals."

"Oh, spooky," Frank jested. "Do the police now hunt after bizarre creatures in the woods? Is there a special department for that?"

The captain glowered at him, not quite sure if he was being mocked.

"Back to the issue at hand," the big man in the stain coat called back. "The polls are coming up two weeks from now. How do we handle McArthur? He has the governor on his side, and his popular vote continues to grow."

"We've got the people on our side," Aunt Randa boasted. "I still have the majority, don't I?"

The talk continued on from the coming polls to the press, to the ongoing corruption investigation on the present governor, then back to the polls again. They talked well into the night, while May picked listlessly at her food. Ed stared morosely down his plate while Frank had glass after glass of wine.

It was nearly midnight and the table had long been cleared before she was allowed to leave. Aunt Randa walked her guests to their cars while May took the chance to retreat to her room. It had been a long day, and she was so glad it was over. She thought of how nice it would be to call in sick tomorrow. She struggled facing the world without Sam being in it; there was just nothing else good about this crappy little town. She curled up under the sheets, wishing time could stand still, and that she could just lie there forever.

* * *

It had been the worst day he'd had in a very long time.

Maybe the worst day of his life.

Sam's mind was still foggy from the jumbled-up memories. May was really upset when he didn't show up like they had agreed upon, which he could understand. He could remember clearly that he had been right by his home before drifting off. He had made a fire and fantasized about all the things they would do together as he stared at the orange-red glow dancing before his eyes. Eager for what new fun they might have.

He remembered going outside to take a piss, and then, then it got foggy. He couldn't remember what happened next. He only remembered waking up out in the woods, which wasn't the first time, to be fair. He had no memory of the time between though; that was unusual. And as much as he tried, he couldn't recall anything else on his way home.

He'd been extra careful not to get distracted by any lights again the following day, but he had failed. It all happened again, and he still had no fucking idea of how. Every time he tried to call May, it went straight to voicemail. He stumbled up the wooden stairs to his cabin, exhausted in spirit, mind, and body. He put his key in the door and immediately tensed up, finding it was already open. He edged the door open slowly, hearing the familiar creaking of the wood.

Inside, it was dark but through the gloom, he could see a vague outline of his furniture, and a humanoid form lounging on his bed.

"May?" he asked while reaching up to light a lantern.

"Welcome home, Sam," the shadow said. He couldn't see their face, but he heard the smile in their voice. He recognized the voice of the woman. She was reclined on his bed completely unclad, with one of his large fur pelts wrapped loosely across her mid region. In her hand, he saw just before it flicked on, a large electric lamp.

"You?" he asked. His brain was already growing itchy, as if his subconscious already knew what was about to happen. "What are you doing here?"

"I wanted to see you Sam, *really* see you." Dana rose, the last cloth protecting her modesty slipping off her chest as she activated the light. In her hand, the lamp illuminated, glowing with a sinister pulsating green light, far stronger and brighter than the earth ever spat out. In an instant, his mind became a jumbled mess, he could barely muster the focus to think a sentence at a time. All that mattered was the dark green glow.

He didn't even have the faculties to worry about transforming, about the way his eyes shifted and grew across his face, or the chill leaving his body as his fur sprouted. There was only this moment, the earth was speaking and it was his place to listen. Dana was laughing in manic disbelief but he barely heard it; still, it reminded him of her presence. Enough to mutter one word, one fear stronger then any other currently lingering in his human side.

"M-May," he groaned, drawing a shuddering breath. "May's coming I . . ." he trailed off, utterly consumed by the lamp.

"Now? Ah shit that's . . . we'll go to my hideout, nobody will find us there," she suggested, as if she was actually conversing with the staring mothman who swayed on his feet in silence. His lack of an answer didn't deter her. "Can . . . can you fly us there?" she asked excitedly, coming closer without regard for her nudity. "It is further north."

She was stunned by how quickly he obeyed. His newfound strength was evident, with his height now nearly a foot taller and his frame much bulkier. She felt his power when he effortlessly hoisted her from the floor to his chest with one arm, as if her weight didn't faze him at all.

It didn't dull the excitement that he immediately transformed, or that they were blasting against the icy air at what must have been driving speeds at least. The wind whipped at them, far more intense than the rides she'd taken on her motorbike, the warmth of his furry body guarding her from the elements as she shouted to speak.

"I-I can't believe it! I can't believe you're really a . . . that you're different, like me!" Her smile was wide but wrong. With his eyes locked downward, even in flight still focused on the bright green light cradled against her breasts. It almost looked like he was focusing on her, listening to her speak. Despite everything, that gave Dana hope. "I had another freak literally in my bed but we never found out about each other; it's crazy isn't it?" she continued. "I'm so stupid, such a coward. I should have told you, but you should have told me, too, right? So it's all okay, we're together again and we know now, that's what matters!"

Sam struggled to hear her words. To understand what was happening and where he was going, and to hang on to his fear even as difficult as that was. Everything but the glow was so soft, so muffled, like chatter in a room separated by a thick wall, even the massive towering trees that he whipped through barely earned a glance.

"STOP! STOP STOP STOP RIGHT HERE!" she shouted, drawing in a breath with the speed of his sudden halt. She huddled against his body, vibrating with the force of his wings as she got her bearings. "There it is, right down to the right, the decrepit-looking place."

They landed with just as much force, the impact shaking Dana but the feel of cold earth under her bare feet sobering her quickly. The shack was indeed decrepit, with warped rotten wood, but it had four relatively sturdy walls. It also had a padlock which Dana quickly unlocked with a key she had hidden nearby. Inside wasn't any more remarkable, but it had a bed, some food and batteries, plus the bug-out bag containing some clothes, a few thousand bucks, a crank radio, and some survival gear.

Sam followed the lamp inside.

He nearly crashed against the wall when it was flicked off, a flood of sensation and memory crashing into his skull as he braced an arm on the filthy wood. The key points were easy enough to recall, that he flew somewhere unknown and more importantly, that Dana knew everything. He took an uneasy breath as he looked up at her, blushing faintly as he remembered or perhaps re-noticed that she was naked.

An old space heater had been flicked on in the corner by her, as well, producing a faint red glow.

Hopefully one he could ignore.

"Dana, how did you—" He stopped; obviously May had told her, or at least tipped her off somehow. "Why did you bring me here?" he asked instead, his voice low and fearful, even though he was clearly stronger than the woman he was looking at.

"I told you, did you not hear me when we were flying?"

"Dana, I'm barely a person when I'm that close to a light that bright; I don't remember shit!"

"I . . . I'm like you; I'm, fuck it, I'll show you," she said, taking a deep breath.

Her eyes grew and shifted, until they were lidless orbs like a pair of blue, fist-sized sapphires glowing on each side of her head. Sam found himself staring at them. He barely even saw as her bright blonde hair turned dirty-white, a tangled mess of fuzzy gray fur. The hair appeared all along her body, up her neck, over her head, and ended in a sharp widow's peak between the two eyes that held his stare. In place of her soft, pink lips, there was a wide suckered maw gap, a cluster filled with needle-like teeth.

The mouth seemed to hiss as she spoke.

"See!" she called, her same old voice there under the static.

"Oh my God!" he balked, frightened but unable to look away from the glowing eyes so close to his face. He had no idea. No idea about Dana or even that creatures like him, albeit of a different type, existed! It was startling and he definitely had more questions, but still, one thought lagged in his mind. "Dana, we should talk about this; we will, but I need to get back home. May will be there soon."

"Forget about May; she's fine, she's *normal.*" It was easy to hear the envy, the venom even as she spat out that last word as if it burned her tongue. "Sam, you should be with me, we should be together; we *were* together, I . . . I was just too much of a coward to tell you." She shifted back to her human form as Sam's uninterrupted staring began to unnerve her.

"I understand why you didn't, Dana," he assured, relieved to no longer hear her hiss. "I mean, it was casual, what we had, wasn't it? It didn't last long either."

"I know, I know! Because you couldn't visit me at night and I was nervous to come out here but now *we both know why!* It was because we're both freaks a-and we should be together," she tried, taking a sweeter tone as she came to brush her own form against his.

"Dana, you know I'm with May."

"Forget about May!" she screeched, squeezing his firm shoulders as her eyes bored into his hazel orbs. "She'll be fine, Sam; she's normal, she's pretty, she'll find another boyfriend in no time!" Dana babbled, coming closer still as her arms wrapped around him. "I need *you*, only *you*, and y-you need me, someone like me, right?"

Sam pulled her off of him as gently as he could. It didn't help the faint red glow and all the brushing up against him was making him hard, something the beautiful blonde no doubt noticed. The masculine, primal part of his brain wanted nothing more then to pin her to the floor and fuck her right now. A dark but fascinated part of his mind wondered what offspring they might produce.

There was only one way to find out . . .

NO!

"Dana," he said more firmly, holding her at arm's length as she stared up at him with those lost, broken, puppy eyes. "We'll talk about this later, maybe with May, even? Still, we're done; we're not going to be together like that. I'm sorry," he offered genuinely.

She looked ready to fall into a heap and sob at the words, but it still seemed the best note he could leave on.

He was just about to push open the door when the green came back.

"No, no just . . . stay here. I need . . . we *need* each other," she tried, hugging him again even as the fur sprouted over his body. How could she make him understand? Why did he have to be so difficult? Why didn't he want her!? She'd fantasized a thousand times about finding the perfect mate, one who was different like her but lovable enough to settle down with. It was a frequent but unachievable fantasy of hers, thinking she was the only one of her sort. She was sure he must feel likewise, even if he didn't want to admit it. To be with someone who could truly understand him and what it was like to be different.

As he turned around to stare at her, or rather the lamp in her arms, she smiled.

She hugged him, trying to get that feeling of closeness she so desired. As she pressed her body against his, she could feel his erection. The transformed state seemed to make him more primal in many senses, and the red light in the corner spurred him on even more.

"Oh? This sticks around, even now?" she teased, trying to revert to the flirty seductress that had first got him into her bed. "Sit down!" she commanded, delighted and deluding herself further as he immediately complied. Positioning the lamp as she knelt to mount him on the dirty wood floor was awkward, wedging it between their bodies was unpleasant and setting it beside her turned his gaze in a powerful reminder.

She placed it directly behind her and that worked well enough, returning her eyes to the massive golden orbs in front. It was almost like he was looking at her now. He was certainly responding to her actions, to the feel of the warmth between her legs against his massive, strange cock, larger than that of a normal human. He groaned as she rubbed against it.

A noise almost like a pained gasp escaped her lips as she began to lower herself upon it, feeling the overwhelming force of the penetration and the strange ragged texture of his member filling her up.

It was bigger than when she'd fucked him before, even larger than Tony's. The sounds he made as she raised her hips and slowly let herself slide all the way down the shaft spurred her on.

"Yeah? You *like* this, don't you?" she urged and panted as she sped up. She smiled blissfully as either of his enlarged hands came to hold her hips firmly, guiding her and holding her in place as she rode him.

The groans and manly grunts under her spurring her on; the sound of his voice in rapture, lost to her for so long was ringing in her ears again. That was all that mattered.

She let herself get consumed by the animalistic force with which he pursued her. His movements grew bolder and more erratic. She felt the heat steadily building up inside her, while her nails bore into his chest. A moment later, it all exploded and the overwhelming climax seemed to consume her entirely. All her senses melted together as wave after wave of absolute bliss hit her. Her eyes opened wide as she cried out in pleasure and her muscles contracted. Her cramping legs squeezed hard around his lean body before she let herself fall onto Sam's furry chest.

"Mmmm, oh Sam," she panted with a smile, while pushing her still trembling body back up again. "Cum, fill me up Sam," she urged him as she pulled away wet strands of hair from her sweat damped face. But he didn't cum, he just continued to pierce her with a steady pace and force.

"It's all for your own good you know" she promised, "so that we can be together. Can't you see that Sam?" When he didn't answer she put her hands around his neck, lifting his head to look him in his eyes, desperate for that emotional connection she so craved. His unseeing eyes felt like a punch in the gut. She threw down his head against the floorboards and slapped him in the face while breathing heavily. His eyes turned toward her, but still without noticing her.

She hesitated a moment, then turned around and switched off the lamp she had placed behind her, leaving them cloaked in a soft darkness, disturbed mainly by that insistant red glow from the corner. She turned back to observe the half naked mothman shrouded in silky darkness on the floor under her. She could already distinguish the fuzzy fur retracting into his skin and his contracting eyes slowly returning to lucidity.

"Sam?" she pressed. He let out a jagged groan, sounding as if in pain as his hands fell away from her to the floor limply. He was naked except for the unbuttoned plaid shirt that constrained his cut biceps. She observed his chest and strong abs, heaving under her.

He seemed disoriented and out of it, but his erection had not faded. She picked up the pace, continuing to ride him faster and faster, enveloping him in her wet warmth. It worked. Only a few moments later, he exploded in her, letting out a muffled groan while seemingly slowly coming to his senses. He blinked and then tried to focus his now attentive eyes on her face. This time, she knew it was really him in there. She smiled as he pumped his semen in her. Perhaps this could make them one . . . perhaps then Sam would understand that he was meant to be with *her* . . .

"Dana . . . what the fuck . . . what is going on?" He stumbled on his words, fighting to understand where he was and what was going on. Fragments of vague memories raced through his aching head.

"Oh God, Dana, what have you done?!"

CHAPTER 19

The knock came in the darkness of sleep.

May stirred sleepily and adjusted the blankets where her leg had slipped out. The room was cold, but she was warm and cozy in the bed. She liked the darkness; it mirrored the emptiness she felt — cavernous and unending. Yet, when she dreamed, she could shape it into anything she desired. She dreamed of her old home back in Roxton Borough, of her small pink room behind the peach trees, of her mother. She sank deeper into the soft cashmere coverlets of her bed.

Rap-tap

This knock was louder.

"Go away, *please*," she muttered. She wanted to sleep and hide from the world just a little longer. She wrapped her hands around her knees and folded herself into a tight ball under the sheets, shutting her eyes tighter, willing her subconscious mind through the darkness, back to the memories of her old Boston home when life was much simpler.

She heard a faint clanking of keys followed by a brief rattle of the doorknob. *Why won't they let me be to sleep my life away?* She groaned and buried herself deeper into the feathery softness of the bed. She heard the sudden jerk of the handle and the laborious creak of the door as it swung open. "Please go," she muttered to the soft footfalls traveling past her bed in slow measured thuds.

She heard the rustle of the window draping and a white glare pierced through the darkness of her eyelids. The light was bright and insistent and forcing her eyes open. May groaned and lifted her hand to shield her face. "Please go away," she pleaded again. "Just let me sleep!"

"Young lady, you've slept long enough. You need a meal and a wash," a voice came from somewhere above. "My word, look at this room." Suddenly her blankets were gone, and the sheets snatched off, thrown into a heap on the floor. She hugged herself tighter and shivered slightly from the sudden blast of cold air.

Seeing no further point in resisting, she sat up and opened her eyes fully. She squinted from the bright sunlight that streamed through the open windows, then looked at her discarded clothes, which were still damp and muddy. The wet, soiled heap was joined by other scattered clothes, sheets, and undergarments littered all over her room. On the couch and bedpost, shoe rack and windowsill, there was even a navy blue brassiere hanging from the ceiling fan. There were mud smears and shoe prints around the threshold, and her bedding lay strewn on the side of her bed.

Standing in the midst of this chaos was Maggie with her arms crossed and a mild grimace on her homely face. She looked around the room and shook her head in disapproval.

"What is this, now?" she asked in her soft, whispery voice. "You trashed your room? This won't do, May, this won't do at all," she spoke gently, her voice filled with sympathy.

May buried her face in her palms; the light still hurt her eyes and she couldn't stomach any form of scolding at the moment. Not even one ever so gentle. She feared an emotional outburst that this poor employee didn't deserve.

"I'm sorry," she blurted out quickly, her voice hoarse and grating.

"Are you alright? May?" Maggie asked, leaning in slightly.

"I'm alright," May flinched, pulling back into the bed. She was not ready for any form of sympathy. She could already feel the tears welling up behind her eyes.

"Okay then, if you insist." The old woman straightened. "You should head downstairs and get something to eat; you barely touched your meal last night." She glanced briefly at the room again. "Best spend at least an hour at the breakfast table, I'll need that long to sort this place out."

The smell of breakfast met her on the serpentine stairs that led into the living room. She took a deep breath of the warm, comforting aroma of deep-fried bacon and eggs, freshly baked bread, and the sharp sweet smell of apple pie. Her belly grumbled and her mouth watered as she descended the stairs.

She found Frank sitting alone on the sumptuously set table nursing a steaming cup of coffee with his breakfast. He was pale and shivering under his black velvet pajamas. Though he smiled when he caught her staring, showing off gray eyes that were pale and watery.

"Good morning, Frank," she said, taking the seat beside him.

"Morning, May," he returned, his voice sounding oddly nasal and hollow.

"Are you alright?" she asked, regarding him closely. "You seem a little hungover."

"Yeah, no shit," he replied, taking a careful sip of his coffee.

She turned to the array of food on the table and picked up a slice of bread. It was still warm from the oven and slightly sticky from the butter. She spread a thin layer of mayonnaise and took a savoring bite. It was sweet and slightly chewy, with a bit of nuttiness just the way she liked. She reached for another slice, realizing she was starving.

At that moment, Ed arrived and entered with Mary in tow. He was clad in baggy blue jean trousers, red sneakers, and an army green shirt that brought out the strange color of his eyes. Mary hovered behind him, looking almost beautiful in a knee-length sapphire blue dress with splayed sleeves and a pleated skirt. She seemed squeamish as she stood beside him, looking furtively at any sign of movement from the balcony above.

"Brother!" Frank called. "Up so early!?" he asked, rubbing his eyes. "And Mary? What a pleasant surprise, come have breakfast; the bacon is *mouthwatering*," he declared, seemingly with no intention to touch his own. Ed turned to regard his twin with cool, calm eyes. One of the few times he didn't seem angry was when talking to him, as brief and rare as those bouts were.

"I've got something important to discuss with our mother." He looked up at the winding stairs. "Is she up yet?"

"Something more important than breakfast?" Frank asked aghast, ignoring his brother's somber tone. "That's quite unlikely," he added with a careless shrug. "But seriously, whatever you might want to discuss with her, I would guess it's something best said after the meal, don't you think?"

Ed loitered behind the stairs landing with Mary fretting anxiously beside him. After a while, he pulled her to the table to take the opposite seats from Frank and May. He seemed unusually tense. His shoulders and arms were stiff, and Mary looked on edge to the point where the smallest excuse would send her sprinting like a startled rabbit.

It was not long before Aunt Randa appeared from the upstairs lobby clad in a voluminous navy blue cloak that somehow managed to make her look stouter than she already was, a rather astonishing feat, really. *The fat old cow always threatened to overflow her clothes,* May thought. Even in the early morning, she was covered in layers of makeup. Her lips glowed a bright crimson on an uncannily manufactured makeupcovered face. The air was suddenly saturated with the sharp, pungent scent of her citrusy perfume.

She paused at the table long enough to cast a quizzical look at Mary through her glasses, then pulled out her chair and sat down without a word. Even May could feel the tension around the table. Mary sat stiff beside her boyfriend, looking as pale as a corpse. Beads of sweat glistened off of Ed's forehead, and neither had touched the food even to make themselves a plate. Frank slurped his coffee noisily while studying the fretting couple over the steaming mug.

Aunt Randa broke the awkward silence after a minute or more.

"I see we have a guest this morning?" she commented between bites of her fried bacon. "Son, is there a reason your friend is here at my breakfast table?" she asked Ed, her eyes never leaving his girlfriend. It took a few seconds for either to answer.

"Yes, Mother, there's something we need to tell you," he replied. He turned to Mary, taking her hand, and in a deep breath announced. "Mary is pregnant, Mom. I know that *you know* that I don't care about marriage, but if you'll give your blessing, we'll agree to be married in the church. Quickly, so nobody has to know about anything out of wedlock even," he offered.

May choked on her slice of bacon.

Frank coughed to keep from gasping.

Only Aunt Randa kept her composure completely, resting her chin on the knuckles of her steepled hands. She stared at her son with an unflinching gaze that seemed to stretch forever, all while her face remained expressionless. Then, her lips curled into a thin ghost of a smile. May was surprised that she had not *yet* exploded.

"How much?" she asked in the tone one might use at the fruit store to ask the price of an apple.

"Ma'am?" Mary asked, quivering under her gaze.

"Mom," Ed growled defensively.

"How much?" Aunt Randa repeated. "How much does it cost for you to fuck off and leave my family alone?" May watched her aunt's face. She seemed calm and composed on the outside but under the tranquil façade, May sensed a brewing rage that was on the edge of eruption. Mary must have sensed it, too.

She went pale.

"No ma'am, I never planned . . ." she stammered. "Me and Ed, we . . . we love each other." She glanced at him for confirmation. "It's not about money, ma'am."

"Then what was it for?" Aunt Randa demanded. "Why did you choose to bring this shame to my home? Why do you want to drag our good reputation through the mire?"

"Chill out, Mom," Frank interjected lightly. "It isn't the sixties anymore, nobody cares if your kid marries a poor person," he gently pressed.

"You will be quiet, boy," she rounded on him. "Or I swear to God, you'll find a new home by tomorrow!"

He threw up his hands in exasperated surrender before finally filling his mouth with the now-cold bacon on his plate.

Aunt Randa turned back to a terrified Mary.

"Why are you doing this?" she demanded. "Did someone pay you? Did my opponents? Was it James McArthur or his people? He's too cunning to do the bribing himself." She was shaking with anger now. "Name your price, I'll pay it. Just take the money and disappear."

"Mother, I've been with Mary for nearly a decade, do you really think she's a spy?" Ed groaned out. He was already subdued by his mother's verbal onslaught. Looking utterly defeated as he put his hands in his face. "We only came here to let you know. You know we don't need your permission to do anything!"

"Oh, shut up, Ed!" Aunt Randa cut him off. "Have you no shame? Letting yourself be blackmailed by this little gold-digger to extort your own family!" She turned back to Mary. "Should Maggie get my checkbook? How much?" she asked in a clearly condescending tone with each word dripping with hate.

Freckle-faced Mary found her courage and a bit of color. She pulled herself up proudly in her chair and even smiled at the old hag's face. "To pay off my love for your son," she said in a tremulous whisper, "there's not enough money in the world." She sniffed softly and used a hanky to wipe her runny nose. "But to leave your life forever, for you to never see me again? That'll be five-hundred thousand dollars."

May choked on her bacon. Frank stared, slack-jawed in astonishment. Ed looked like he had been shot in the chest, vulnerable for maybe the first time May had ever seen as his eyes widened. Only Aunt Randa was unsurprised. She called for her checkbook while smiling a bright red grin filled with the sweetness of relief, and a deep sense of bitter triumph. Ed was fit to gag with the veins bulging from his neck and his face red with anger. He seized Mary by the shoulders.

"What are you talking about?" he asked, almost shaking her as he gripped her arms. "You're taking money to leave me?"

"Do you really think this is the first time she has tried to pay me off?" Her laugh was thick with misery and bitterness. "I've turned her down at least three times already, but I can't fight off your family, Ed. I'm leaving."

Maggie arrived with the requested checkbook, and Aunt Randa wrote the check with a smug smile, muttering happily to herself. Despite losing so much, she was clearly the only person in the room visibly pleased by the unfolding of events. Amidst everything else, May was staggered by the amount of money she'd just spent.

Mary ripped the check from Aunt Randa's grip with a stoney, unwavering expression. She examined it closely and slipped it into her bag before walking out of the house. Silence lingered in the room long after the door slammed shut.

"So," Aunt Randa said after the long silence, "Now that we've gotten that out of the way, can we go back to our breakfast like a normal family?" she asked with a sneer.

Ed pushed back roughly from his chair. He pulled himself up to tower over his mother. "I *fucking* hate you," he growled through clenched teeth before rushing out of the house. A few moments later, they heard the dull thud of his car door and the loud roar of the engine as he drove out of the yard. After his lover maybe? May wanted to think so.

Aunt Randa watched him leave with barely veiled distaste. Her lips parted as if she wanted to speak, but she swallowed whatever she was about to say. Frank pushed off his plates and stood up, looking somber for maybe the first time since May had met him.

"I seem to have lost my appetite," he said. His soft words only wounded May further when he grabbed a bottle of wine off the rack and tucked it under his arm before disappearing into the main lounge. It took a moment for May to even clock that she was left alone with a bad-tempered Miranda Baker. The fat woman snorted in disdain and returned to her bacon.

"My two sons—a drunk and a fornicator," she muttered to herself, "So has the Lord seen fit to teach me humility? Moral decay of our children is a big cause for concern for the country now, I suppose." She turned to May. "But not you, dear. It seems Helen did a good job with you; I trust you're still a virgin, right?"

May almost choked a third time by the abrupt question. The question that took her completely by surprise and left her briefly flustered. She felt her aunt's eyes from across the table, intense and expectant as she regained composure. She chewed, swallowed, and managed a timid nod.

The sharp, tender silence lingered for the entirety of their breakfast.

It was a full hour and a half before she climbed up the stairs back to her room. Breakfast had been far too exciting for her liking and left her craving the secluded solace of her little sanctuary. The safety of solitude. The room had been arranged by the time she returned. Her clothes were even sorted and neatly arranged in her closet. The soiled ones were packed into a laundry basket and ready for the dry cleaner. The redwood floor had been polished to a high sheen and the whole room permeated with a mild scent of lavender and rosewater.

God, they weren't paying Maggie enough.

She found two large cardboard boxes on her bed which were sealed with masking tape, but easy to open. The first box had old clothes that were damp and musty with disuse. The second was filled with old books. The small storybooks were bright with colored pictures. There were also big, voluminous novels with hardbound covers, tucked in with old magazines and other odd assortments.

Termites had been feeding on some of them.

A particular book caught her eye, and she picked it up. It was a large paperback album with vivid pictures, portraits, and stamps. She studied the images. One was of a brown-haired girl with dark grayish-brown eyes. There was a slight familiarity in the face that gave her pause. She struggled to ponder the place and name, but she just couldn't.

May continued to flip through the pages until she was interrupted by a knock at her door.

"Come in," she mumbled. The door opened tentatively, and Maggie entered. She struggled with the weight of another large box until May rushed to help. "What are all these?"

"It's the worst kept secret in town," Maggie replied. She sat on the edge of the bed. "And since you're a Baker on your mother's side, it's probably best you know, too."

May stared curiously at the old lady.

"What secret?"

"Maddison Baker's, she is named after your grandmother; she's the girl in the pictures,"

May studied the brown-haired girl closely trying hard to recognize her. She could be anyone in a crowd. She turned back to the woman asking for answers with her eyes.

"Maddie is your cousin, May," Maggie elaborated. "Frank and Ed's older sister. She was such a pretty, lively child. You would have liked her. This house was never happy again after she left." May looked around. "This used to be her room."

"What happened to her?" May pressed, desperate to know.

"Your Aunt forbade any contact with her after she left, but last I heard, she had moved to Europe with her husband and their newborn daughter. Maybe you should talk to Ed; he'd know more. Frank might, too, I suppose, though they weren't as close."

As if Ed would tell me anything, May mused. *It's no wonder he seems to hate me.* The revelation still shocked her. No one had ever told her about Maddison Baker or any other Bakers except the three she already knew.

"Why did she leave?"

"For the same reason Mary left this morning. For the same reason your mom left. The same reason your aunt now bears her father's name. It's the curse of the Baker Woman."

"You knew my mom?" May asked. "When she still lived here?"

"Yes, May, I did," Maggie replied with a solemn smile. "I'm old. I knew your grandparents back when this family still ran the mill and bakery."

"Wow." May smiled. "Mom never said anything about that," she defended, immediately regretting it.

Maggie looked wounded.

"She never mentioned me? Not even once? I practically raised her and your aunt."

"Well," May began, trying not to offend any further. "She hardly talked about her childhood at all, to be fair,"

"I wouldn't blame her," Maggie said with a profound sadness in her voice. "It was a dreadful thing, what they did to her, poor child." May frowned and remembered the reverend from church. This was the second time someone made reference to her mother with such melancholy.

"What really happened to my mother?" she asked while she turned to face the maid on the bed.

Maggie stared a long time at the wall as if the answer was engraved on it.

"Love happened," the old woman said simply. "Your father did. She met a boy and brought him home. Your grandparents would not accept him. He was only a *negro* lumberman from Wood's End, hardly a fit partner for the heir to the Baker's holdings," she wrung her wrinkled hands and rubbed one over the other. "I failed her. That night she got up and ran off with that young man. A few months later you happened, and you know the rest from there, I imagine."

Maggie left abruptly, leaving May lost and confused but giving her time to process her thoughts. How long she sat on her bed in shock, she didn't know. She looked at the three boxes still lying beside her, her mind raced back to the years before she had arrived here, to the missing sister. To the other family member who was in all likelihood about to disappear with his lover and half a million dollars for the exact same reason.

Concerns far more serious than a scummy, cheating boyfriend.

What could she do?

CHAPTER 20

At dawn, the country air always seemed cold and wet, and today it had a ghostly mist shrouding the large steel pavilion at the central square. Frank stood beside a crowd of campaigners with his hands tucked deep in the pockets of his blue leather jacket. He watched the damned commotion through sleepy eyes and wished he could be somewhere darker and quieter. In other words, basically, anywhere besides here.

He would have still been in his room at that moment, in his soft bed, wrapped under layers of warm blankets if his mother had not been such a bother. With her recent falling out with Ed, the sole responsibility of maintaining the family normalcy had fallen squarely on his less-than-willing shoulders. With the elections in less than two days, maintaining the family image had never been more paramount to his mother.

As if she needed an excuse to be excessive.

He didn't give half a fig who succeeded Mayor Wellington for the mayor of Springdale. Still, a lot had fallen on him and May to carry on with the last days of the campaign. He could see her standing at the front of the pavilion with a large banner and a superficial smile plastered on her face. He made his way through the mass of election aids, walking up from behind to stand beside her.

"What are we even doing here?" he asked, uncharacteristically despondent as his breath steamed visibly in the cold air. The main entrance to the town hall was across the street from them and barely visible through the thick foggy curtain. "I don't see the point of any of this; it's not like we need the damn money. All the job does is stress her out."

May didn't respond. Her eyes remained fixed on the wall of clouds around them. Her cheeks were flushed red from the cold as her breath came out in small puffs of steam. She looked fresh that morning in skinny blue jeans, a soft pink cashmere sweater with a matching pink beanie, and sneakers to boot. Her long black hair was oiled back and bound with a matching pink ribbon.

"You know, I tried to catch fog the other day," he offered, trying to force a reaction. "I mist," he said with a laugh. Again, May didn't respond. *So much for familial company.*

He stood silently beside her for a little while watching the sunlight break through the mist as it shone down from a somber sky covered with gray storm clouds. He wished for a quick end to this farce, and a big bottle of gin, so long as he was making wishes. Still, he didn't leave. He stood there in the damn cold with his hands in his pockets and that flat look that always came so easy. Even after she completely ignored him, he didn't budge, seeming content enough with the awkward silence. His presence grew on her nerves, it chafed at her like the upsetting thoughts in her mind. Ever since the conversation with Maggie, Maddison

Baker hadn't left her thoughts. She needed to get the whole truth and fuck it, she wasn't going to get a better chance.

"Frank," May called. "Who's Maddison?" She faced him immediately after asking to see the flustered look on his face before he composed himself.

Busted.

"Where did you hear that name from?" he asked, turning away from her stare.

"Does it matter?" she asked. "What matters is that I've been here for months, and no one has bothered to mention her name."

It was his turn to feel the weight of silence. His eyes were fixed ahead, but she could sense the sadness in those orbs mixed with a hint of annoyance. Or was it anger? He tensed as she continued speaking.

"Why didn't you tell me you have a sister?" she prodded.

"You never asked?" he replied simply. "Besides, she's nothing to you."

"Except for the reason your brother despises me," she countered, her emerald eyes narrowing. "But who can blame him? His sister leaves home under difficult circumstances, and here I come, barely a year later, gallivanting in to take over her room," she chuckled sourly.

Frank shook his head, sighing.

"Oh no, no, it's not your fault Ed is raging," he objected. "My mother's too high a target and I am too, let's say, inconsequential," he chuckled. "So, when you arrived, sweet and innocent as you were, he finally found someone to blame for Maddie, I guess. I really do think it was all subconscious though." He took another deep breath. "Ed has always been angry. Even as a boy, he was prone to bouts of rage and would spend hours in his room brooding over little offenses, but . . . he used to laugh, too, you know? He used to be a normal person." May just stared, perplexed.

"Then what happened?"

"Maddison happened," he replied gloomily. "I was his twin, but Maddie was like a mother to us. What I imagine a mother's supposed to be, at least. Maddie would read to us, bake him walnut cookies. She would leave her door open whenever our mother was out of town so we could sleep in her room. We would creep into her bed at night and snuggle against her until morning when the storms scared us." He grew a warm smile without meaning to. "And boy, she could sing. Her voice was meant for songs, and she would sing to us every night before bed. Growing up, Ed loved to hear her voice. I think that's why he took a liking to Mary. She must have reminded him a bit of Maddie even though they look nothing alike," he joked, blinking back tears as he continued.

His breathing was hard and short. May watched his chest heave and huff as his breath exhaled giant gusts of steam in the cold air. She waited patiently for him to compose himself.

"She was smart, kind, and dutiful. Better than any of us could have asked for." A single clear tear rolled down his cheek before he brushed it off. "And one day, she was gone, disappeared from our lives just like that. It broke something in him that's never been fixed. It broke me, too, honestly. You might have noticed I drink a wee bit more than I should," he joked bitterly. He looked away as if her very image was too much for him to bear. The mist in the plaza was clearing, and they had something of a view at least of the surrounding forest.

"Have you tried contacting her?"

"How?" he scoffed. "Do you have a way of speaking to the dead?"

"Dead?" she echoed, her mouth suddenly feeling dry. *Oh, that is so much worse!* "Maggie told me she moved to Europe with her new family!"

"That's what we tell everyone who cares enough to ask." He turned a deep shade of red. "Europe . . ." he laughed miserably. "The truth is she got pregnant, they told her she could either kill it, or she could hit the bricks without shit from her family except the clothes on her back. Then she killed herself. It's been a year since then, and I haven't spoken about her until right now."

May felt her head pulsating. *Worst kept secret indeed.* She almost laughed in astonishment.

"Does your mom know about this?" she asked, trying to suppress the horrifying suspicion blooming in her mind. "Does she know you guys lie about what happened to your sister?"

Frank gave a hearty chuckle, but his eyes were as angry as Ed.

"Know about it?" his voice whipped. "The lie was her idea from the start, and she made us sell it to everyone else. 'Pick a side, loyalty either to your family or to a dead sister.' Our father was the only person who would stand up to her, but even he had been helpless. No matter how he tried to broach it, she wouldn't budge, and he was too broken to try for long,"

A father, too. May mused. *Of course they had a father.* She recalled the phone conversation she had overheard in Aunt Randa's room the first day she fought with Ed.

"Matt, right? He's your father?"

He looked at her, almost shaken from his sorrow by the surprise.

"Matt was a piece of shit," he said hotly. "He's not fit to be called anyone's father. He left my mom when Maddie was still a baby, and when Ed and I were only bumps in her belly. He's a big-shot politician in Florida now, Senator Matthew something."

Is there no end to this? May despaired.

"What other father do you mean, besides Matt?"

"The one who raised us," he replied with a mild grimace. "Mom's second husband, Marcus. They were together almost my whole life but . . . he couldn't handle my mom's growing obsession with public opinion. The situation with Maddie was the last straw. He couldn't live with the lie my mother demanded, so he left. Mother forbade contact with him, too."

"Why? Why would she reject the memory of her own daughter?"

He looked directly into her eyes.

"Take a wild guess."

"It would ruin the family name?" she guessed, disgust in her voice.

He gave her a knowing solemn smile.

"And now you have your answer," he said simply. May turned back to the town square where the bulk of the crowd gathered. *Her own daughter.* She felt her anger growing with a rising sense of indignation. Children should come before public opinion or any selfish political ambitions, dammit! She was angry for Maddie, for Mary, for her own mother and Ed, for the arrogant prejudice that had made their lives so much harder than it had to be. She wanted to hurt Miranda Baker, to get back at her, however she could.

She let the banner drop from her hand. An idea forming in her mind, something that would hit Miranda Baker where it hurt her most. She walked out into the open square, over to a certain man with a press hat. Frank walked alongside her inconspicuously.

Through his gritted teeth, he asked, "And what do you think you're doing?"

"Picking a side," she declared, stomping off with fixed eyes on the group gathered beside Town Hall. They proudly hoisted banners and placards into the air, calls to vote for *dear* Aunt

Baker. May joined the crowd in the open plaza, calling out to the reporter loudly, unconcerned with whoever may overhear.

* * *

He felt weak and shaky lying on the floor under her. She wasn't heavy, but her blue radiant eyes gleamed with mad determination. He tried to pull away, but she reached for his member and started to run her fingers along the shaft rapidly. "No, Sam. You got to stay with me," she panted. Dana swayed her body and her heavy breasts danced in front of his eyes. Her tangled blonde hair spread over her shoulders as she returned to her stunning human form. Even now, he felt his cock stiffen against his will, and saw that she definitely noticed it.

Still his mind was screaming at him. This was not what he wanted; he loved May and he knew how much this would hurt her. She was the one and *only* one for him. He made a sudden effort to get up, making Dana topple over on the floor from the surprise. Her eyes narrowed. "Sam, you're being ridiculous; think about what's best for you! *We* should be together we-we're the same! Forget about May." Her words became desperate as she reached for the lamp and switched it on, capturing his attention before he could make a dash for the door. Sam stopped dead in his tracks, turning his now glowing golden eyes toward her again.

She smiled. "There we go," she whispered.

Sam heard her voice as a faint echo far away. He tried desperately to hold on to reality and not drift away again, but as the green light approached, it consumed him again.

Dana felt him relax, and despite everything, it was a great relief.

After making him lie down, she took his hands and guided them to her breasts as she pushed herself against him again. She felt his hard member against her leg.

175

Suddenly, one of her feet accidentally knocked the lamp over, and Sam's eyes immediately darted away from her direction to followed the light with his eyes. The lamp ended up to the left of her instead of behind her, and she was painfully pulled out of the pleasant delusion where it was only him and her and nothing else mattered.

His focus was most clearly *not* on her.

A jolt of desperate anger bubbled up in her chest. He was gonna be hers; she refused to give up. She wasn't letting the first freak she'd ever discovered slip through her fingers! She wouldn't be alone again! She was not going to lose control, but she needed him to see her. For real. She grabbed some rope in the corner of the cottage and securely tied each of his wrists to a wooden post. She then went back to straddle him, and closely observed his face while she turned off the lamp once again . . .

* * *

It was midday when the long-threatened storm broke heavily and suddenly from an overcast sky.

May was at the clinic for her first shift in some time when she saw Tony appear around the corner. His dark hair was plastered limply on his face and dripping water on the marble floor. *Look who the storm blew in,* she mused gloomily, trying her best to act normal while other people were present. She had no time for his lewd stares and easy smiles, but thought it best to play along. He could jump between two modes in an instant, charming and flirtatious, or completely consumed by a dark, untamed hunger he had no intention to control unless someone else was present.

"Here you are!" he said with his smile still in place. "I was wondering where you'd been hiding."

"Excuse me?"

"Well, you've been gone from your desk for almost a week now and it had me wondering."

"Oh." She glanced away, having a hard time looking at his eyes. "I've been busy."

"Too busy for a drink? A hot chocolate perhaps?"

"No thank you," she answered hastily, his stare making her uneasy.

"But I insist," he pushed, offering her a pleading smile. "A good hot cup of brown might just be what we need to warm you up after a day like today. Who knows, you might end up warming up to me" He reached for her hand.

"Hey! That's close enough!" she snapped, flinching from his grasp. "And I would thank you for not touching me please! I've had a really bad afternoon without you hovering over me. And no, I don't think a bucket of chocolate could warm me up to anyone right now," she seethed.

Thankfully, he recoiled from her sudden outburst. His arms flashed up as if to block a blow but seemed unfazed by her sudden aggression. She watched his face contort as a brief spasm of anger flashed in his dark eyes, followed by a deep, brooding frown. It was further relief that her sudden outburst had attracted a few curious glances from other refugees in the room. She saw the color rising on his cheeks as he stared at her with narrow, dark eyes.

"Sorry, sorry," he repeated, not seeming very sorry at all. His gaze averted sharply from hers, and as he noticed the glances from around the room, his tone softened. "I never meant to offend."

She laughed dryly at that.

"So, uh, Dana's not been at the clinic for even longer than you. Her line has been inactive too . . ."

"That's weird," May remarked, suddenly concerned. "Has anyone filed a police report yet?"

"Not that I know of. I don't think she has any family in this town, and no one seems to know much about her here. That's uh . . . why I was here, to see if you'd show up today or . . . maybe her," he commented.

She was about to press further when Frank appeared through the open door, shivering under a large umbrella.

"It's time to go, May," he called to her. "Mom came to pick you up!" She was already on her feet when she remembered that morning's revelation, and the thought of getting into a car with Miranda Baker wasn't appealing. She turned back to Tony. "I've changed my mind," she said hurriedly. "I think I'll have that hot chocolate now."

* * *

Where was he . . .

Sam lifted up his head slightly and looked at her, blinking to collect himself and focus his gaze in the dark. To try to think over the splitting migraine all the lights had summoned. He tried to move but realised that his hands were tied. She was sitting over him, and with a crooked smile on her lips, she grabbed his shoulders with both her hands and gripped him tightly. She leaned in close and let out a slow, hot breath in his ear. Then she whispered, "Tell me you want me, Sam. Tell me I'm the only one for you." Sam took a deep breath and coughed. "Tell me, Sam," she repeated in a honey-sweet whisper, one with a blatant undercoating of danger.

"Dana, please . . ." he begged. "I can't."

With a sudden motion, she slapped him hard in the face. He saw her bobbing breasts in passing as his head followed with her motions and his ear started to ring. She began choking him in her delirious rage. Under her, she felt his cock twitch, and a terrifying smirk bent her lips.

She lifted up her ass and slowly slid her pussy back and forth over his half stiff cock, letting him feel her wetness. When she let go of his throat again, she grabbed his now-stiff member and slowly guided it inside her, reveling in how Sam's body reacted to her.

"Tell me you want me, Sam," she whispered in his ear again. "It should have been us two, you know. Don't you remember what I did for you? All the fun we used to have." She could feel his hard cock twitch inside her and observed his face.

"No! For fucks sake, Dana, please. You have to let me go!" he pleaded.

"Tell me," she urged him again, sitting up and staring into his eyes with a look Sam could not interpret. Dana started moving her hips up and down, leaning on his neck as a support and restricting the oxygen to his brain, making him dizzy. She alternated between enveloping him completely, and lifting her hips until only the tip remained in her. Her hand didn't budge until she felt him starting to shake under her. Then she finally let go, revealing red marks where her fingers had been. He desperately tried to catch his breath, but as soon as he managed to take one deep wheezing breath, she gripped him again.

"Tell me you want me Sam, tell me we are going to be together!" she urged him. She alternated between clawing at his body, choking him, and kissing him while whispering soft words. She became visibly more and more deranged and desperate as his response remained conspicuous by its absence. Once again feeling the frenzied movements and spasms as his body was screaming for oxygen, she let go, sitting back and observing his frantic attempts at sucking in as much air as possible.

"I love you, Sam," she whispered. "I will take care of you. I understand you, you know. No one else can understand you like I can. Please!" She started kissing his dry, cracked lips, his shoulders, and chest. Moving downwards toward his abs, and kissing his member. She let the tip of her tongue slide along his shaft, licking and cleaning his cock with her mouth. It was damp both from his own previous climax and her fluids. She started moving downwards, sucking, kissing and licking. Working herself down toward his thighs, legs, and feet, before moving up again. She felt his body shaking, exhausted and drenched in sweat, the salty tinge mixing with her own slightly sour taste. Even now, Sam's cock reacted to her treatment.

He cursed himself. He loved May. Dana had visibly lost it completely, but he could not help his body's reaction to her. Quite literately, he had no control over it.

His body glistened with sweat and her hungry, wanting eyes seemed to devour him. She grabbed his cock, working her hand up and down while feeling it stiffen under her fingers. She guided it inside her again, teasing only the tip with small motions, then suddenly sitting down all the way, enveloping him completely. He let out a groan as his muscles tensed. She held out her right hand, seeing Sam flinch. But instead of hitting him, this time she carefully caressed his cheek, moving her finger tips over his face with a light touch. She felt him slowly relaxing again and breathing out, almost as a sigh of relief. She leaned down and put her forehead against his, looking him straight in his eyes. "Sam . . ." she whispered with a cracked voice, filled with pain and sadness, "tell me we will be together, you and me."

Sam felt his entire being almost paralyzed, too exhausted and disoriented to talk. Should he give in to her demands? He closed his eyes and saw May's face in front of him. Her smile, her rosy cheeks, and her cute little nose. He gathered his last strength and tried to shake Dana off, giving a last desperate attempt to show her what she was doing, to remind her he was a prisoner. He saw how a fire of madness started to burn in her eyes. She grabbed him by the hair, pushing her forehead against his.

"TELL ME YOU WANT ME!" With overwhelming force, she screamed at his face, letting out all the frustration that had bunkered up inside her for so long. All the loneliness, doubt, and sadness. She started choking him while Sam felt small droplets of her saliva hit his face as she unleashed on him. He tried to fight back, but could do nothing with his arms tied. He was feeling his strengths leave him and his field of vision becoming smaller and smaller as he wondered if this was where he would die. Dana refused to let go, seeming completely lost to her inner demons. That was the last thought that drifted through his mind when all things became black, and the world disappeared.

* * *

The election results were being announced on television.

Miranda Baker sat on a couch directly in front of the wall-mounted TV set. She was surrounded by her campaign staff and faithful party members. May watched from the back of the lounge while standing on the lower steps of the serpentine stairs. She sensed the rank anxiety permeating the room, mixed with the light odor of sweat and wine. Everyone held their breaths as the reporter called out the ballot.

She recognized familiar faces in the crowd. The big balding man who had dinner with them a couple of nights ago stood by a slender one with nervous gestures. She watched the sad-eyed woman who had worn the emerald-green dress, and the man beside her who seemed to be her husband. At the far side of the room, Frank lounged on a blue chesterfield sofa far away from the throng of TV watchers with a half empty wine glass in his hand, precariously leaning, but she didn't see any sign of Ed. He had still not returned to the house since the incident with Mary, not that anyone seemed to care.

A steady buzz of excitement grew as the results were announced. May saw a portly, red-haired woman in a long gray coat turn around to cast a curious look at her. She tapped the man beside her and leaned her head toward May. Then he did the same with the man standing next to him. Before long, half of the room was staring back. Her angry eyes darted from the TV screen to glare accusingly at the crowd.

On the screen, May wore a big smile while staring at the smiling face of that flabbergasted reporter. She remembered that moment. When she cheerfully aired all the dirty laundry she'd recently learned about the daughter driven to suicide and swept under the rug drew particular disgust.

On the stairs, she turned back to the crowd, to the scores of accusing eyes turned against her. She noticed their condemnatory stares, cruel mouths, and wagging tongues. All she heard was the loud noise echoing in her head like a large swarm of bees. A primal warning of danger. The room had suddenly grown too hot for her. The air was stale and suffocating. She whirled as she exited the room and walked up the stairs, seeking the blessed privacy of her room. From the lounge, she could hear agitated voices steadily droning on and on. On and on until a loud crash cut them off, bringing even May to her feet.

CHAPTER 21

May dreamed of the little pink room with the peach trees again. The home of her childhood, where she last felt truly safe, happy. She woke up feeling strangely empty, with a larger vacuum in her chest than she had felt in a long time.

The room was dark. For a brief moment, she tried to recall where she was. A part of her mind was still in the dream, which was painting images of the old Boston address; as her eyes adjusted to the room, she remembered where she was. The old manor.

She climbed out of bed and waddled downstairs with bare feet; it was dark outside and the whole house was silent. Still half asleep, she couldn't guess the time. Dawn and dusk looked much the same this time of the year. She found Maggie in the dining room setting up the table for a meal with a hassled look on her weathered face.

"Hello Maggie. What time is it?"

"Almost dawn, just a few minutes past six." Even without seeing her face, May heard the anxiety in her voice.

"Maggie, is something wrong?" she asked. "Where's my aunt?"

It must be about her.

"Your aunt's at the hospital," Maggie said in a whispery, strained voice. "What you did on the TV . . . The election ballots . . . well for starters, she lost, May," Maggie sheepishly informed her. "I suppose it was too much for her to take, and her heart gave out." The words rang hollow in her head. *What a week this was about to become.* May stuttered but failed to ask her question. "She's not dead," Maggie answered as if she had read her mind. "Only hospitalized at the county hospital. Frank called last night and said she had a shot at recovery, at least. He's there with her now."

May collapsed in her chair, dizzy with emotion. Her attempt at vengeance cost Aunt Randa the election and maybe her life. *Did something good actually come of political sabotage?* As rotten as it made her feel, wouldn't life be so much easier, so much gentler, if that woman never left the hospital? Ed could be with Mary, everyone could discuss the sister they missed so dearly, nobody would have to wear a fake face.

The overwhelming guilt had strangely enough not robbed her of her appetite. Her belly grumbled at the prospect of food. She inspected the plates on the table. Set for two, she couldn't fail to note. *I thought it was just me in the house.*

"Yes, it's breakfast for two," Maggie replied, seeming to read her mind again. "Ed came in not long ago. I think he means to leave again before Mrs. Baker, or Frank, return from the hospital."

Not before I've had a word with him. May rushed up the stairs, breakfast vanishing from her mind. She paused in the narrow lobby and listened for sounds through the closed door. Silence spurred her to knock twice but she received no answer. She tried calling out, but only silence lingered. She wondered if Maggie had been mistaken when the door suddenly jerked open and she jumped backward from the surprise.

His eyes were bloodshot and she was hit by the rank smell of alcohol. From his unsteady bearing, it was clear he had been drinking,

He stood in the narrowly open door, his eyes like chips of flint in a blank emotionless mask. Her heart thumped as she met his gaze. *Why didn't I plan out what to say exactly?* she desperately scolded herself.

"Hey Ed!" she tried, keeping her tone jovial. "It's nice to have you back." His face was stone before she spoke, and still it hardened. He muttered something under his breath, whether a greeting or a curse she couldn't tell; she didn't really hear it. Instead, May tried a different tactic. "Won't you come down for breakfast?" she offered. "Maggie made walnut cookies." His love for the nut-flavored cookies was common knowledge in the house.

"I'm not hungry," he retorted, turning his back to shut the door.

As he left, May blurted out without thinking.

"Wait!" Ed halted and turned to May, exasperation in his eyes. "I know about Maddie; I know what happened to her, and I know it was unfair" The words tumbled desperately out of her mouth. "No one should have to lose their sister that way, and I can't blame you for being angry; I-I would be angry, too." She took a deep breath. "You can't keep holding on to her. You *must* be so tired of being so angry all the time. I'm sure she'd want you to be happy, too!" She stretched her hand as if to touch him but stopped short.

His face hardened further *still* as she spoke. Hot anger blazed in his eyes as he bored down on her. At that moment, she feared he was going to actually hit her. Thankfully, he only growled and shut the door in her face.

"Stay away from me!"

She felt oddly calm as she walked down the stairs. He reacted as expected, if not as she hoped, but she felt lighter as she climbed down for breakfast. She cleared her conscience, the proverbial load lifted off her shoulders. From the dining room, the smells drifting up actually brought a small grin to her face.

That lasted until she saw the short policeman on the porch. He wore a brown uniform with a copper star. On his shoulder sleeve was the sewn-in metal badge that marked him as one of the deputies.

"Good day, Miss Sandler!" he offered with a slight incline of his head and a boyish grin. "I'm Lieutenant Desmond Dolt of the county police. I'm sorry to disturb you so early in the day, but there's been a report of a certain Dana Patterson and a . . . Samwell Sullivan. Both are reported missing, and apparently both had relations with you?"

Sam.

With all that'd been happening at home, she had barely had time to think about him. She did her best to keep a straight face. Inside, she was wracked with fear.

"Dana is my colleague at work and Sam is my . . . um . . . my boyfriend," she blubbered before turning red. "But I haven't seen either of them since Dana stopped coming in to work two weeks ago . . ."

"Okay," the officer replied, scribbling notes on his small notepad. "Just don't hesitate to contact us if you have any information that can help. We'll contact you if we have further questions. Until then, please don't leave town. Your uh . . . *boyfriend* is the prime suspect; he's had a few brushes with the law and the folk here," he warned, spinning around and walking back to his truck in the yard.

May felt a cold dread engulf her. It occurred to her then what hadn't before, that nobody in the police or otherwise in this town was going to go looking for Sam if he went missing. If something happened to him. Nobody was going to find him passed out by the mailbox or the road. Goosebumps rose under her skin as a shiver crept up her spine. Tony had mentioned Dana's disappearance from work, but she assumed that Dana's nonchalance was behind it. *But Sam seemed to have fallen off the planet, too, all in a short span of time . . .* There was something sinister going on, and she was determined to find out what. If something indeed had happened to Sam, she would not be able to forgive herself if she abandoned him like all the others.

* * *

May was eating breakfast when Ed came down from his room.

She watched him shamble lifelessly into the dining room as he tilted precariously on his heels. He lurched unsteadily into a seat and grabbed for a loaf of bread.

What had he been doing with himself?

She watched him drunkenly tear out a chunk, chew, and swallow. Often, he'd pause, breathe deeply, or even cough with his mouth full. It made him seem likely to retch at any time. She derived a twisted satisfaction in watching him torture himself, but still something made her speak up.

"Ed, listen . . ."

He cut her off sharply.

"Don't even say it," he demanded, raising a hand in protest. "I know what you're going to say. And yes, you're right. I'm

187

better than this, but I don't care" His voice was filled with emotion, even with his face hidden behind his long, grimy hair. "Yes, I'm tired of being angry, but I can't just stop." He wiped snot from his nose. "Fourteen months, May . . . Fourteen months and not once have I spoken to anyone about her. All because of one woman's selfishness," he laughed. "Well, on the off chance that fat fuck lives, I'm leaving this house. You'd leave too if you had any sense."

"You couldn't possibly believe that," she argued. "You wouldn't have stayed this long if you had completely given up on this family. You can still have your family without her," she suggested, seeing a flash of doubt in his crazed eyes. Ed scowled as he spoke.

"And even if I'm willing to try and I'm not saying I am, what makes you think she'd listen? Mary and I are taking the money and leaving; we're gonna start a new life, make a new family, a real family," he insisted. "The only reason I stayed this long was a spot in the will, and I hate myself for that now. Even if she dies, even if she hasn't already edited me out of the inheritance and I finally get to stay here, in my childhood home with Maggie, my twin, my love, even if *everything* works out like I'd hoped. It wasn't worth it."

May found herself struck silent. Ed had never spoken so much or so plainly to her. Now he had, and seemed willing to say more, all while looking her in the eye. She found herself completely dumbstruck. In the end, they talked for hours, almost until noon; he cried a few times as he horrified her further with all manner of tales. Talk of the abuse they'd suffered, talk of the happy times with his beloved sister, talk of mischief with Frank and how much he missed his stepdad.

It was a difficult talk, but she knew it was good for him.

CHAPTER 22

The blood red motorbike was parked in front of the bar. The building was ramshackle with a long narrow frame, pale green lichen, and visible cracks on the old cement walls. Bright neon bulbs erratically flashed at the adjacent street lights, which enhanced its sinister ambiance. May emerged from the car while scanning the darkening street. What little sunlight slipped through the clouds had long vanished into the western horizon. A few stars had already made their appearance, twinkling down like polished diamonds.

It was past dusk, and the bar favorites were making their appearance as well, arriving in cars, taxis, or simply emerging from dark alleys and deserted back streets. May stared at the squalid drinking hole; an uneasiness washed over face and dampened her lips.

Dana almost bumped into her while coming out of the front door of the dollar store beside it, startling her sharply. She carried a large cardboard box in her hands, loaded with all manner of supplies, walking briskly with her head down. She even jerked when May ran up to her, the box dropping and spilling its dry groceries on the tarred ground.

"May," she said, looking visibly disconcerted. "W-what are you doing here?"

"Nothing. I was just out . . . looking around when I saw your bike parked here."

"Oh," was all the other girl could manage. She got on her knees to gather the various bags and cans that had gone spilling.

"How have you been?" May asked cautiously, crouching down to help. "There was a police officer at the house. He said someone reported you missing," she pressed. Dana let out a nervous chuckle, trying to sound casual as she replied.

"Oh, must be that dolt, Tony. Horny bastard's been blowing up my line nonstop for days now," she explained with a laugh. "Do I look missing to you?!"

"No, you don't," May acknowledged. "But I think Sam might be. No one's heard from him in weeks. He's not been out by the intersection selling flowers; I can't even find him in the woods at his house." She studied the other girl as she spoke. Dana had never looked so unsettled; her long, tangled hair was slightly matted with mud and spruce needles. She struggled to act calm even as her eyes widened further as she visibly unraveled. May noticed her wincing even when she heard Sam's name specifically. "Have you heard anything about him?" she finished, boring into her eyes.

"I don't know!" Dana said too quickly, not looking back at her. "He's your boyfriend, not mine!" she defended, gathering the last of her things and hurrying away. "Take care, May. Sam's a grown man. If he's missing, maybe it's because he doesn't want to be found . . ."

May watched her drive off into the dark as her suspicion grew beyond any doubt. *What have you done to my Sam?* It all made sense now, the familiar woman's voice on the phone that day. Her absence and unruly behavior. *That thieving weasel.*

May didn't know what she had done to him; but whatever it was, it clearly wasn't good. She needed to find him urgently. For his sake, she couldn't involve the police; they wanted to arrest him for squatting already. She needed to do this by herself.

* * *

May stared at the woods' edge and studied the long, somber tree line. They stood tall and solemn, the dark green needles and narrow leaves rustling in the morning breeze. Layers and layers of tall green conifers stretching on forever it seemed.

A light snow was falling, which lowered branches with weighted down water and coated the forest floor with a cracking carpet. She shivered slightly as a tiny flake drifted through the air to settle on her nose and other patches of exposed skin. The last rains of autumn had come and gone; winter was here.

May had spent half the night deciding whether or not Dana was somehow linked to Sam's mysterious disappearance. The other half was spent contemplating where Dana might be hiding him. She knew now it was somewhere in the woods. Wood's End provided ample cover for anyone who wished to avoid the prying eyes of others.

The question was, where? The woods were huge to begin with, not even factoring the concealing abilities of its caves and overgrown bushes. The spruce needles in Dana's hair last night narrowed it down to the darker, rockier parts of the forest where the tall, looming evergreens grew, but even that was a hell of a wide search area.

Still, wherever Sam was, May was determined to find him. Worse, it had to be today. Before she left town, a search party had been assembled at the town square to clear out the forest; to finally get rid of the witch and/or hobo that was *somehow* ruining the woods with their presence.

She walked into the woods and stayed close to the pines and spruces. While no expert, it wasn't that hard to follow the trail in the snow left by Dana's bike. She was dressed warmly, but the wind blew hard, and bitterly cold, piercing through her thick coat. Her shoes were caked with snow and mud, and her feet numb from the cold as she pressed on. Snow crunched under her feet as she followed the winding rocky path through the trees.

The little flurries ceased after a couple of hours and a few rays of sunshine hit the forest floor, making it breathtakingly beautiful. As the snow thawed, glistening green grass emerged while small icy rivulets trickled away. She continued along the narrow footpath leading straight ahead. It periodically appeared and disappeared through fallen needles and ankle high undergrowth, but she hadn't lost sight of her trail yet. May needed her answers, wherever the path would lead her.

The morning was spent before she spotted an unfamiliar little shack through the trees. It was an old tumbledown cottage propped up by a small, rocky outcrop just beyond the tree line. Not the first she'd spotted in all her time out here. Most likely, it was just another abandoned home of the lumbermen who once worked in these parts.

But Dana's bike was parked outside, right at the end of the trail May followed.

She approached the building warily with her eyes scanning the nearby trees and bushes for any sign of movement. There were no windows on the structure, and the only point of ingress sat at the front door. She found it locked with a solid deadbolt shackling a pair of rusted clasps fastened to a termite-eaten door. For a moment she hesitated, then she heard a familiar, low groan.

It was easy enough to find a rock she could use to smash the hinges. Completely unconcerned with the loud noise that echoed through the forest with each blow, she attacked the padlock furiously until it broke and fell to the ground.

May pushed open the door and was immediately enveloped by an overwhelming conflagration of bright lights. A sinister glow of deep green, pulsating like a living heart of an emerald beast. Through the blinding glare, she saw a vague humanoid figure on its side.

"Sam?" she asked, taking a wary step forward, squinting to see in the overpowering light. The figure raised its head.

"May?" the voice sounded hoarse and painfully strained, but it was unmistakably Sam's. "The lights May . . . turn it . . . turn off . . . hurry" He raised a weak hand toward another corner of the room. May found the switch and jammed it down, plunging the room into a deep gloom. She rushed to Sam just as he tried to pull himself up and collapsed face-first to the ground. She was in shock to see how thin he had become as he morphed back to his human form. His cheeks were sunken in slightly, which emphasized the sharp bone structure and prominent brows. His eyes flickered open as she touched him, his pupils unusually bright and dilated.

"May, I'm sorry," he breathed weakly. "Dana, she . . . she . . ."

"I know! I know!" May cried, wrapping her arms around him. "I tracked her here."

He shook his head.

"May, she's . . . she's . . . not just . . . she's dangerous" Every word was a struggle for him, but she heard the words; the words he desperately worked to tell her. He clutched her hand. "Dana, she's . . ."

An angry hiss made May spin around, her heart skipping a beat.

Dana or something that had *once been Dana* stood in the door opening. She was clad in the same black leather jacket with matching latex pants May had seen in town. It was likely the only reason she recognized her. Inhumanely large, glowing blue eyes, the strange fur that barely resembled her hair, and the *teeth*.

It was the teeth that horrified May.

The mouth opened and hissed again. A furious, sizzling sound escaped out of the disturbing flaps in her neck and the side of her head. The gleaming, sapphire eyes locked on May. It lunged at her while gnarled clawed fingers waved around maliciously. May waited until it scrambled a few feet toward her before she moved her hand.

She gripped around a short piece of wood that had broken off the door on her way in, and swung wildly, putting all her weight behind the strike. The blow took the raving creature in the temple, sending Dana crashing against the open closet.

She saw her opportunity and pulled an exhausted Sam to his feet. She put his arm around her shoulder to support him, desperate to get him out before the police found the same trail as she had followed, and reached the shack. They were already past the door when the creature spoke. When *Dana* spoke.

"Wait," came the grating voice from behind them. "Don't go," it wheezed.

May wanted nothing more than to leave those woods and never return, but something made her stop. She wanted answers. She turned around as the creature struggled to its feet. The hair above its left ear was matted with green blood where the blow had landed.

"Just wait," it rasped, or begged; it was hard to hear Dana's voice under the static hissing noise.

May waited to listen but kept a wary distance between them. She had one arm around Sam to support him, the other still clutching the piece of wood tightly in her free hand. Glowing blue eyeballs stared back at her from within the dim room.

"Don't leave, May, don't take him" The grisly maw barely moved with her wheezy cries. "I can't stand to be alone anymore!" The gaping mouth quivered as it spoke. "You don't need him, too, I have *nobody!*" she shrieked. "Since I was just a little girl . . . Since . . . Since they took my family from me . . . I've been completely alone in this world! There was nobody else like me, nobody else I could tell everything, nobody I could be me with!" she desperately begged. "Then . . . Now . . . I've found someone who's different like me. I just . . . I just wanted him to be here with me but . . . I'm so stupid! I ruined everything!" Her voice broke into sobs as she crumpled to the ground. "I couldn't let him leave or he might tell someone." She hesitated before adding "and I really wanted him to be with me; I thought that perhaps I could convince him to leave you and be with me instead." She took a haltering breath, her words seeming to fully devolve into a strange crying.

May stood, gaping and at a complete loss for words. *Was nothing ever what it seemed in this wretched place?* The response came from Sam.

"You don't need to be alone, Dana," his voice strained. "I know what it's like to be alone, to hide your identity from people out of fear of rejection. But you're not alone, none of us are." His tone was oddly calm, and without venom, much to May's shock. "We're not going to tell anyone about this, how could we?" he added, with a grandiose wave at the strange prison shack. "I could forgive you for doing something crazy, maybe even May could, too eventually?" he half-asked, turning his gaze to her.

"I . . . fuck, Dana I don't know what I expected but it wasn't this. I don't even know all the details of what happened. I need answers. But . . . look we'll talk about *all* this later, right now we have to go. Police are searching the woods as we speak" May urged with a slight panic in her voice.

"I think this is a good time to go visit my family, don't you?" Sam asked, joking despite the splitting pain in his head. It was worth it to see half a smile on May's face. "Dana, come on, you'll be safe there, there . . . most of them are like me. Besides, you'll need your head treated!" Dana watched them leave, up until then motionless, aside from the quivers with her sobs. Sam's words raised her head up, though it was hard to read the expression on the horrific face. May kept an eye on her as she crawled to her feet, and followed them out.

May was duly grateful for Sam's indulgence, to her own surprise, she felt more pity toward Dana than ill will. When people were desperate, they were capable of crazy things, that was a fact. Maybe for some it brought out the good and others, others might do something utterly *insane* like kidnap a friend and keep him prisoner, apparently.

Well, maybe she felt a *little* ill will toward Dana. With any luck they'd be able to put all this behind them, but first, they had to escape the mundane shit. The law was coming. It was with that in mind that Dana spoke up again.

"C-could you . . . could you endure being a moth just a little longer? So we can fly away?" she asked, holding one of the industrial battery lamps up weakly.

CHAPTER 23

It was three days before Sam was back to normal, and it would be longer still until Dana's cracked skull was fully healed. At least she was well enough to call in and confirm she hadn't been kidnapped or murdered. That would draw some heat off Sam hopefully. Both were safely resting up at Sam's childhood home after some . . . creative explaining. Leaving out the bits about romantic obsession, and the fact that she knew Sam the person *before* Sam the mothman, made Dana's little abduction forgivable to his kin, it seemed.

Oh, how many 'kin' there were.

Sam hadn't mentioned that the apple orchard he grew up in was a subsection of a massive family farm, one he shared with multiple grandparents, a half dozen aunts, not to mention more siblings, nephews, nieces, and cousins than she could keep track of. The place felt more reminiscent of a beehive than a moth nest, especially with everyone bunkering inside for winter. It didn't help her social anxiety how many were utterly fascinated with 'little Sammy's' first girlfriend, especially when topics as innocuous as 'how she liked Springdale' and 'do you have any family' were so touchy.

May had only just escaped the breakfast table and Sam's ferociously friendly mother. The plump old blonde lady was such a striking contrast to her son, who seemed to take after his father best she could tell. Her host was chatty, excited, and above all, *loud*. Still May liked her; she was supportive and cheerful even when it was brought up how far away they might be moving.

All the same, May was eager to get outdoors, even in the cold.

The sky was dark gray with light flurries drifting and dancing in the gentle, frigid wind. Outside the gate and fencing, something emerged from the shadows that were against the fence. May rushed through the snow to a dark male figure under a bare-branched apple tree, tackling him in a happy hug.

"There you are! Feeling better?" she declared, sighing into his arms. Sam chuckled. That noise, and seeing him on his feet without struggle, made her squeal in excitement. An action which made him blush yet harder. *It was good to hear him laugh.* He pressed the three white flowers he'd managed to find into her hand rather than answer her question.

"They're beautiful," she declared. "So, have you thought anymore on our next move?"

He shrugged.

"Springdale is done with me, and I'm done with it. I can always build another cottage somewhere else, preferably someplace where camera phones don't work, one of the dead zones out west, I'm thinking. It'd make strangers a lot less scary if I didn't have to worry about getting caught on a livestream. There are a few towns you find completely unconnected out there; I figure we visit those until we like one, then setup somewhere a half-hundred miles out into the forest or something." He flashed a melancholy smile. "It'll be a lot of work though."

"We'll be smart about it, and besides, you have two extra sets of hands this time!"

"Not to mention the cash you and Dana saved, and the fact you're two nurses," he teased. "We'll practically have the makings of our own little commune," he leaned in to plant a soft kiss on her forehead at that. No more words were needed; May had never felt so content. Never had she been so excited for the future than now, while he wrapped his arms around her. The gray, half clear sky shone diamonds from above as the snow danced gently around them. "How's your family holding up?"

"I . . . I'd like to check on them, and introduce you, maybe?" she tried.

"I'm fine with that; I don't care what your family thinks of me."

"I'm sure they'll love you, most of them," she mumbled, guiding him by the hand away rather than elaborate. Springdale had a better camping store anyway; they wanted to swing by for supplies before disembarking, and it was a chore they could do while Dana kept resting up.

There were a small fleet of cars to borrow, though they ended up hitching a ride with an eerily quiet woman not much younger that May, a sister who volunteered eagerly to join them but said nothing on the ride. Sam didn't seem concerned, and even hugged her a second time after drop off. She could ask about that later though; there was all the time in the world to talk about his family, not less so with the upcoming road trip.

Besides, it wouldn't do to start a conversation steps away from the old house. May entered without knocking, she'd texted Ed before coming, Frank and Maggie too, just to be safe. To her surprise, all of them, and Mary, were eagerly waiting for them. Frank surprised her the most.

"Is uh . . . my aunt out of the hospital?" she asked, unable to hide the concern at the sight of him.

That soured the air just a little, but the clean-cut twin smiled as he replied.

"No, not for a long while they said. She's stable though, for now, if she ever does go somewhere besides a hospice, she's going to need constant care though."

"Oh I . . . I'm so sorry,"

"I ain't! She gave me power of attorney over everything, old hag isn't going to throw out my new sister or nephew ever again!" he declared, pulling Mary against him with a little half hug. "Just need to figure out if she knows how to contact my dad, and I'm ready to stuff her in a home to rot."

May found herself staggered slightly by the cruelty he was speaking with. Even Mary looked a little uncomfortable, or guilty. Still, she couldn't really judge, not after all she'd heard from Ed about their childhood, all the neglect and abuse inflicted by the fat woman. Even speaking logically, she'd much rather the assets be here with her family then whatever politician or hate group Miranda was planning to will her millions to in place of disowned children.

Her family.

That thought almost slipped by her; she found that she truly thought of the people here with her as family. Ed, Frank, Sam, even Maggie and Mary had grown a real place in her heart. With that smile, she managed to bring it to lighter topics. To the unbelievable dates Sam had taken her on, to the fun nature facts he could share with them, and the actual pleasant childhood memories the brothers shared.

Then they discussed their upcoming plans to build a new home.

There were mixed reactions to the last bit, but the family all at least claimed they were happy for her. From their talk segued to the trip they were making to the nearby camp supply store and Frank quickly volunteered to drive them. Oddly, he also seemed to move immediately, almost rushing them out the door.

He applied similar enthusiasm filling up their cart inside, buying all manner of crap that Sam gently tried to protest, the most exciting of which was a solar-powered chainsaw that was to replace her boyfriend's ax. Nobody could argue that it would save them a shitload of time. It was expensive though, and even if the family was rich, it felt awkward to have thousands of dollars spent on her by the man she'd only known a few months.

It made his last little act of generosity all the more striking.

"Ah hell no, I'm not moving all that heavy crap again!" he protested, shocking May as she looked at their cargo in the back of the truck. It was true that he, and Sam, were still sweating from that little chore, all the more unpleasant with how cold it was, but still! She'd only asked if he wanted them to unload it here. "My arms are still sore. Nah, you better just take the truck too," he offered casually.

May couldn't even stutter out a response, Sam didn't even try to. Both of them instinctively wanted to protest, but her attention was stolen by the shiny metal flying at her. Frank tossed her the keys, leaving her with a flustered smile and a dazed mind as he turned to reenter the manor.

How long has it been? A year? Less? Half a year about.

So much had happened within that time, more than had happened in the twenty long years she had spent in complete triviality. She'd arrived a young girl, timid and green as summer grass. She would still be the same if not for the people she had met here, for good or ill, they had changed her. Now, she carried them everywhere.

She had come for a job in the clinic, but instead she'd found a friend, a lover, and a family. Were Dana and her still friends? Sam had forgiven her and he was the one most wronged; it was his idea to invite her along even. In any case, she wasn't going to argue with him, she was still too relieved.

She'd found her peace again. For the first time since the little pink room with the peach trees, she felt content, happy. More than that, May felt excited for the future.